D0962628

Praise for Patricia Forde's *The List*

"Compelling to readers of all ages, *The List* is a spellbinding book about language, the environment, and humanity's role in protecting them both... A beautiful and absorbing read you won't soon forget."

—Bustle

"Patricia Forde crafts a richly imagined future society, the development of which feels all too plausible in today's climate... This is a story with a message and a purpose, one full of relevance and originality. Forde reminds us that words do hold power, both to heal and to destroy, and that because of this we should be mindful of how we employ them. This is a love letter to the ways love and art can lift our spirits and replenish our souls in a world that often seems dark."

—*BookPage*

"Forde's exploration of language as both weapon and savior is a noble one, and environmental undertones bolster its power. Pair with Patrick Ness's *The Knife of Never Letting Go*."

—*Booklist*

"An electric sci-fi novel with a strong ecological and moral stance."

—*Bulletin of the Center for Children's Books*

THE
LAST
LIE

Also by Patricia Forde

The List

THE LAST LIE

DANGER
Love run
lie RAGE
TRAP RESCUE
Power
FIGHT ENEMY CUT WARN
ALIVE Voice
BLOOD
TRAITOR moonlight
BURN SECRET
Dangerous
HUNGER TRAPPED CHASE HISS
RUN SPY PANIC
RAGE IMPRISON trap Dream
Love TRAP
WOLF PEACE DREAM
Dance Undercover
TIDE
UNDERCOVER ESCAPE
GRAVEL heart
SHIVER
BUTTER trigger

sourcebooks
young readers

PATRICIA FORDE
Award-winning author of THE LIST

Published by Sourcebooks Young Readers, an imprint of Sourcebooks Kids
P.O. Box 4410, Naperville, Illinois 60567-4410
(630) 961-3900
sourcebookskids.com

Library of Congress Cataloging-in-Publication Data

Names: Forde, Patricia, author.
Title: The last lie / Patricia Forde.
Other titles: Mother tongue
Description: Naperville, IL : Sourcebooks Young Readers, [2020] |
"Originally published as Mother Tongue in 2019 in Ireland by Little
Island Books." | Audience: Ages 10-14. | Audience: Grades 7-9. |
Summary: When the rebels are captured Letta goes on the run, still
striving to preserve language while the vicious new ruler of Ark plans
to eliminate it once and for all.
Identifiers: LCCN 2019058921 | (hardcover)
Subjects: CYAC: Vocabulary--Fiction. | Censorship--Fiction. |
Dictatorship--Fiction. | Science fiction.
Classification: LCC PZ7.F755 Las 2020 | DDC [Fic]--dc23
LC record available at https://lccn.loc.gov/2019058921

Originally published as *Mother Tongue* in 2019 in Ireland by Little Island Books.

This product conforms to all applicable CPSC and CPSIA standards.

Source of Production: Maple Press, York, Pennsylvania, United States
Date of Production: June 2020
Run Number: 5018544

Printed and bound in the United States of America.
MA 10 9 8 7 6 5 4 3 2 1

To the children around the world who are being separated from their families, and to every child without a voice.

CHAPTER 1

#231

HARE

SMALL WILD ANIMAL

The ink was dark and slightly sticky. Crimson. It reminded her of blood. It was made from berries, harvested in autumn, the precious juice extracted when the first leaves began to fall. Letta dipped her nib in carefully, trying to avoid any splashes. The cards were lined up before her. One word on each card. One word from the mother tongue they had all but lost. This batch described wildflowers.

Buttercup. Daisy. Primrose. Cowslip.

Each letter was written in her own cursive script, red ink on white card. She pressed the nib to the card, heard the gentle scratch, the smell of berries and vinegar wafting around her head.

"Ready?" Marlo asked, pulling on his jacket.

"Yes," she said. "I just need to pack my bag."

He waited as she put the cards into their boxes, then handed her the old leather satchel, his strong hands touching hers for a second as lightly as a butterfly touches a flower. She slipped the boxes into the satchel alongside a slim volume of stories. She fastened the straps, enjoying the feel of the old leather and its rich, spicy smell. It smelled of home. This had been Benjamin's satchel. Benjamin, her beloved mentor, who had raised her after her parents went away.

"All set?" Marlo smiled at her.

She followed him across the floor of the old pump house, up the ladder, and through the trapdoor. They walked across the high, dusty hallway that smelled of bats and mold and damp. Marlo nodded to the young man who stood guard, and he in turn looked through the peephole. Letta waited. The boy pushed against the great doors. They swung open, complaining loudly on their rusty hinges. The boy checked that the way was clear outside, then stood back to let Letta and Marlo pass. Letta breathed in the cold air. All around her, the trees whispered in the wind, leaves shivering as the fat plop of raindrops hit the forest floor.

Thirty minutes later, they were walking through the rough grass of open fields. A world of ruts and stinging nettles, of waterlogged sod and winds laden with the smell of damp, earthy moss. The landscape had the pallor of a dying afternoon in winter, with everything and everyone locked in its cold embrace. An east wind had moved in overnight, bringing with it a slate sky and constant showers of wintry rain. Letta and Marlo climbed, hand in icy hand, as the land stretched upward, a slope that was bald and bare from the heavy rainfall.

At the summit, they paused to catch their breath. Below them, Letta could see the dell, with a thicket of small trees and bushes that would hide them from prying eyes. When they reached it, she settled herself, sitting with her back pressed against an old pine tree, the dampness permeating her thin clothes. They had chosen this place because the land had been left fallow. There were no workers to worry about, no reason for anyone to be there. Marlo moved away to stand on a knoll from where he had a good view of the surrounding countryside. Then they waited.

Letta heard them before she saw them. Her ragtag band of scholars. Ten children ranging in age from seven to almost twelve. It worried her that they had come together, that they were making noise. She would have to speak to them again about how important it was that they be careful. These children came from the bravest people in Ark, people who were prepared to risk and lose everything so their children could learn to speak properly. Within minutes, the youngsters were sitting in front of her, eyes wide, waiting to hear what she had to say. She cleared her throat and began. "I'm so happy you could all come this afternoon."

The wind rushed in across the fields, and she struggled to be heard over its eerie whine. It was the raw end of the second month, when the earth is still cold. Thaddeus, one of her youngest students, looked at her with wide blue eyes and put his hand up. In his other hand he held a daisy, its head squashed in his warm palm.

"Letta, what call this f-flower?"

He stumbled over the last word, a non-List word that Letta had only recently taught him. She had a sudden intense memory of picking daisies with Benjamin when she wasn't much older than Thaddeus.

"Daisies symbolize new beginnings," Benjamin had said. She hoped it was true.

"It's a daisy," Letta said.

Daisies in February. The Melting had left the climate in chaos, and nature was still acting strangely. "Can you tell me the names of any other flowers that we learned?"

The small boy's forehead creased as he struggled to remember.

"Primrose, daff-o-dil, buttercup…"

"Excellent, Thaddeus," she said.

He was such a clever boy. He should be in a proper school, she thought, remembering her own days in Mrs. Truckle's classroom, where they had learned John Noa's words, the list of seven hundred words allowed in Ark. They didn't know at the time that they would be the last children in Ark to be offered seven hundred words. After Letta graduated, children were given only five hundred words. And now even that school had closed.

Letta and the Creators did their best to teach those who wanted to learn, though it meant teaching them in the open air, in desolate spots where they wouldn't be discovered. People had taken to calling these gatherings "hedge schools," since they often took shelter under bushes and trees. More parents were trying to send their children, even though discovery would mean death. Letta glanced behind her to where Marlo stood on guard, scanning the countryside.

The wind squeezed through the grove, its breath frigid, and Letta blew on her hands to warm them before opening her little book of stories. It was one of the few things she had managed to take from Benjamin's library before going on the run. The blue cover had once been stiff and inflexible, but now it lay limp in Letta's hands, the pages crinkled and yellow-stained with water. It was older than the Melting, from another time, a time that was almost impossible for her to imagine. A time when books were everywhere, when people churned out stories and everyone was free to read them. A long time ago, before the water levels rose and drowned most of the planet. She opened the book carefully.

"I'm going to read you a story," she said and felt the ripple of anticipation that shimmied through the group. "It is about a mouse who saved a lion."

"I had mouse once, but I put him in box and him die,"

Thaddeus said. "Mama think him not have enough air." The corners of his mouth turned down at the thought, and his brother Aaron hushed him.

"Listen story, Thaddeus," he said.

Letta smiled. She turned to the book again. She was about to start reading when she saw something shoot out from behind a grassy mound to her right. She jumped. It was an animal. Its fur was brown and russet, but Letta saw a flash of white on its belly. It had long ears with white tips and strong back legs.

"Look!" Thaddeus cried. "Rabbit!"

"Not a rabbit," Letta said gently. "A hare." She picked up the book and began to read. "Once upon a time—"

"Letta!" Marlo's voice cut across her words like a whip.

She looked back at him.

"Gavvers!"

Her heart stammered.

"On horseback. Go quickly!"

They had rehearsed this. They knew what to do, yet now the children stood frozen.

"Go!" Letta shouted.

The children recovered quickly. They started to move to the far side of the copse where the shrubbery was dense. Letta and Marlo shepherded the little ones. Letta held Thaddeus's hand. She could feel the daisy squashed between them. When they reached the stone wall at the northern end of the small enclosure, they lay on the ground. All around them, the shrubbery formed a screen. The rough ground was cold and stony, but no one moved. In the distance, the inexorable beat of hooves came closer. Men on horseback. This was a new intervention from Amelia Deer, as leader of Ark. Before this, horses and all other animals had roamed freely as John Noa had dictated. But Amelia had captured and tamed them, and now they made the gavvers far more efficient.

Beside her, Letta heard Marlo breathe in sharply. The horses were getting nearer. Thaddeus squeezed her hand. She caught Marlo's eye and saw her own anxiety reflected. He held up a finger in warning. *Don't move.* They lay totally still as the horses galloped to within a few strides of them. Letta heard the animals snorting, smelled their sweat. She imagined them tossing their heads, pulling on the reins. And then the hare they had seen earlier broke cover and flew out in front of the huge, galloping figures. Thaddeus went to stand up, to stop the little creature. Letta hauled him down, clamping her hand over his mouth.

A shot rang out, and the hare crumpled. Through a gap in the undergrowth Letta saw him fall to the ground. Brown fur on green grass with a halo of crimson. Under her hand, Thaddeus shivered, his warm tears splashing on her fingers. The horses stopped. For a second there was total silence. Letta could hear Thaddeus breathing, her own heart hammering.

"Rabbit!" The gavver's voice was rough and hoarse. "Take it! Give Central Kitchen."

Letta heard a mutter of agreement, then the horses took off, the thunder of their hooves receding, as she pressed her ear to the cold ground.

Werber walked slowly along the beach. The wind whipping in from the sea was cold and punishing. His eyes watered. Above him, the seabirds screamed as they ducked and dived above the boiling waves. He had come to the sea to get away from the tyranny of the big house. Since Noa's death, Amelia had taken him as her apprentice. She had insisted he learn to speak the old tongue properly, though he had felt uncomfortable about it. Noa had always said that language was the enemy, the reason humans had destroyed the planet. But Amelia had explained it to him. Language, she said, was a necessary evil for rulers, though unnecessary for ordinary people. A society needed only one set of ideas, one way of looking at the world. Leaders were charged with outlining what those ideas were. To do that, they had to be able to express themselves fully. Others were not tasked with that responsibility. They only needed to obey.

And so he had learned the old tongue and became a warrior. A Green Warrior. One of the elite champions of the environment who had been with John Noa from the very beginning. Werber lived now to serve Amelia and Ark. Together they had come up with new ideas to control language. Amelia was almost totally blind but never missed anything. She had an amazing brain. He was trusted with even the most sensitive secrets now. He was part of a family.

But sometimes at night he lay awake worrying. What if Amelia discovered what had really happened in the Water Tower? He was so ashamed of his action. He had helped a murderer to escape. Not just any murderer. The person who had killed John Noa. Letta.

He hated Letta. Didn't he?

He stopped to look out at the sea.

He hated her.

The force of his emotion shocked him. He bit down hard on his lip, tasting blood in his mouth. She had made him forget who he really was.

He couldn't forgive her for that.

Carver had told him that she was alive and involved with the Desecrators. She was a traitor, working to destroy all that Noa had worked so hard to create.

She had made a fool of him. He had believed that she was young and innocent. Pure. A person he could spend his life with.

But Carver said that she was rotten to the core. He had to accept that. Overhead, a gull screeched, an eerie, otherworldly sound. Werber shivered, then turned and walked away.

CHAPTER 2

NON-LIST

DANCE

MOVE IN PATTERN,
USUALLY TO MUSIC

It was a year almost to the day since the battle at the Water Tower, and life in Ark had changed utterly. John Noa, founder of Ark, had died that day. He had ruled Ark with an unrelenting harshness, and not many had been sad to see his departure. Almost immediately, Amelia, Noa's partner, had taken power and proven herself to be every bit as formidable as John Noa and even more vicious, despite her failing health. Rumors painted her as feeble and almost totally blind, but that didn't seem to deter her from her mission.

To let the people know that she was now running Ark, she had embarked on a reign of terror. Tin Town, which lay on the outskirts of Ark and was populated by the poorest of the poor, refugees who didn't make it into Ark after the Melting, had been razed to the ground, its inhabitants taken as slave labor or thrown into the forest to be eaten by wild animals. The Creators (or Desecrators as they were still called by the authorities) had gone back into hiding, only venturing into the town when in heavy disguise. Letta, in particular, was a wanted woman with a large bounty on her head.

But there were positive signs too. The Creators had organized meetings in hidden places and talked to the people about freedom. Their following was increasing all the time. Mostly, people were concerned about their children, who were growing up unable to express themselves. They were the first generation without any knowledge of the old tongue. All they had were the five hundred words they had been given by Amelia. Until now, their parents had been too afraid to share the language they stored in their heads with their innocent offspring.

The revolution that day in the Water Tower had shown some people that there was still hope. Some people, but not many. Most people were too terrified of Amelia and her gavvers to see that freedom was even possible. Letta had come to realize you had to have fear to have hope, but you couldn't hope until you left fear behind.

She had been anxious to play her part. She had come up with the idea of the hedge schools, and even though Finn, the leader of the Creators, had been wary of letting her risk her life again, she had insisted. In the end, he had agreed. She loved the children, and their thirst for words was insatiable. But it was an uneasy situation. Letta was constantly afraid that the children would give themselves away by using the words she taught them, or that the gavvers would discover the school and hurt the young scholars. Amelia had shown little compassion since Noa had died. Letta had been consumed with dread and guilt about Amelia being her aunt, a blood relative. But Marlo had reminded her that Leyla had also been her aunt, and she was the sweetest person to ever draw breath. And so Letta went on living in the pump house, taking each day as it came.

The pump house was an old lichen-spattered stone building from the time before the Melting. Its roof was caved in, a home to raucous jackdaws, and its windows were boarded up, leaving it blind to the outside world. It was deep in the forest, miles from Ark, an island of sanity in a world gone mad. Nothing on the outside gave a clue to what lay below ground level. Beneath the building was where Letta and the Creators lived, in a maze of basement rooms of all shapes and sizes.

Life was tense in the pump house now. Security was tight. Finn led this small hunted community with quiet confidence, but for those who had known him before his beloved Leyla had been murdered, he was a changed man. Letta watched him as he went about his daily chores, listening to reports from scouts, discussing what they might eat with the cook, monitoring their supplies of water. And all the time, she could sense an absence in him, a feeling that he wasn't fully there, that some part of him was still with Leyla. Here, inside the walls of the pump house, where there was music and art and laughter and words, it was easy to feel her spirit. Letta hoped she had found peace somewhere.

She still missed Benjamin. She thought about him every day and whispered his name in her sleep. Only the previous night she had dreamed of him. The dream had brought her back to a time in her childhood when Benjamin had taken her to the beach and shown her how the water was giving back what it had taken: every year the sea receded a little. It was an old memory, tattered around the edges, but in her dream, it was as vivid as if it had just happened. When her grief threatened to overwhelm her, there was always Marlo, who held her and whispered comforting words.

It helped. But Letta missed her old life. She missed Ark. It hadn't been perfect, but it had been predictable. She ached to be back at her own desk, knowing that Benjamin was upstairs puttering around, knowing that she had a job to do. She missed Mrs. Truckle, even though the old woman had sided against her and taken John Noa's part. She missed watching her neighbors come and go, full of the hustle of life. She even missed going over to Central Kitchen every day to collect her food.

And she missed her parents. They had left Ark when she was a small child, gone to search for places and people that might have survived the Melting. They had never come back. In all her short life, she had never felt their loss as much as she did now. She missed them with an aching loneliness that she found hard to describe. She wanted to walk to the edge of the sea and look out, scanning the horizon for a boat with silver sails, but she knew she couldn't turn the clock back. She knew she couldn't live a normal life now. She was a rebel, an outcast, and a fugitive.

She knew all of that, but it didn't help. And she was beginning to feel claustrophobic. Finn and Marlo meant well and only wanted to protect her, but some days she wondered if they had forgotten it was she who had engineered Noa's demise. They treated her like a delicate flower, while inside she felt like a bear—an angry bear. The energy that had driven her to stop Noa still burned inside her. She wanted freedom, for herself and for the people of Ark. She wanted justice. She wanted something approaching normalcy, something like people had had before the Melting.

"Are you on dinner duty?" The small dark girl who had asked the question was frowning down at her.

"No," Letta said. "I don't think so."

The girl shrugged. "Must be me then," she said and sauntered away.

Letta stared after her. She didn't like Carmina. She couldn't put her finger on why, but she just didn't. Carmina was an artist. She was responsible for the row of portraits that hung on the south wall of the pump house. Letta's gaze found them now. These were the martyrs, the Creators who had been killed by Noa's regime. At the end of the line, she could see Leyla and

Benjamin. Their faces had a light to them that made them look alive again. Letta often stood and examined Benjamin's portrait, and each time she was even more impressed at Carmina's skill. But it didn't make her like her any better.

Carmina was a soldier as well as an artist. When Letta had moved into the pump house twelve months earlier, Carmina had been living in Ark undercover, a spy for the Creators. She had only come back to the forest two weeks ago and had been hailed as a hero. Letta had felt that Carmina was not happy to see her there, and since then they had settled into an uneasy truce.

Letta turned back to her work. Finn had managed to get her some card stock, and she ran her hand over it, its smoothness reassuring her. There were so many words to record. Some days she felt a wave of panic when she thought about the words she had stored in her head. She had to write them down, pass them on. Today, she would start with this room. She looked around.

Window: A framework of wood or
metal that holds a pane of glass.

Soon, she had thirty words written on her white cards. Once again, the words sang in her head and shot around the room just as they had when she was a little girl. When she stopped to rest, she found she had an audience. Twelve or so children and teenagers were standing around her table. Letta looked up at them. A young boy clapped his hands and smiled. "You know many words. So many."

Letta shrugged. "You are welcome to these if you want them."

The boy smiled. "We will… I'm sorry…" He hesitated. "We will sh-share them," he said. "Thank you."

A girl standing next to him pushed forward. "Do you have word for this?"

Letta looked and saw that the girl had wool and needles in her hand. The needles were whittled sticks, and the wool had been gathered from the fields and the sheep who lived there. For a second, Letta feared that she didn't know the word, couldn't remember it, even though it was circling in the air just beyond her grasp.

"Knitting!" she said. "It's called knitting."

Knit: To tie or link together,
especially yarn or wool.

Letta's heart leapt at the look of gratitude on the girl's face. "Nitt-ing," she said. "I used to know that word. My mother give it me. I forgot. I know I should not have. I know it was a spe-special thing, but I forgot."

Letta touched the girl's arm. "Don't worry," she said. "You have it now, and I will write it down for you so you will never forget it again."

For the rest of the afternoon, Letta wrote words for anyone who wanted them. She had realized a long time ago that there was a huge discrepancy in language among her new friends. Some, like Finn and Marlo, spoke quite beautifully; others, like the girl with the knitting, had everyday language and nothing else; others again had few words and made themselves understood through a mixture of mime and facial expressions.

As Letta wrote words for them, she tried to imagine why this was. Obviously, Finn and Marlo had grown up with educated people who had a great store of words. Others had been separated from their parents at a very young age and forced to fend for themselves.

Many children had arrived at Ark almost feral. An old man who used to visit Benjamin had told her about them. John Noa had taken them in and placed them with families who took care of them. They had recovered in most ways, but their language was destroyed. Most of them had few words, and it was difficult for them to take on new ones. She had met many such people in the wordsmith's shop. People who desperately wanted to speak properly, to be able to express themselves, and Letta's heart had ached for them. And the Creators were no different: they too had their share of people with some words and others who had almost none.

Letta looked up from her work. Finn and Marlo were due back. There had been a demonstration today. Finn had taken a group to the fields to play music for the workers. Letta had longed to go, but it had been decided that it was too dangerous for her. They hadn't had a demo like that for a long time. But Finn had gotten word that there was a training day for the gavvers and that security would be lax. Letta hoped he was right. A week had passed since she'd seen the gavvers shoot the hare. A week in which she was haunted by the sight of them parading around on horseback. Quicker now, and more lethal than ever before.

Carmina had just called people to the table to eat when they heard the trapdoor open.

"Finn!" a child called out and Finn jumped into the room, followed by Marlo and the half-dozen musicians who had gone with them to the fields. Letta smiled. They were safe.

Over dinner, Finn was in better humor than Letta had seen him for a long time.

"It went well!" he kept repeating. "It went very well."

Letta looked around for Marlo and saw him with Carmina, their heads close together at the far end of the table. She felt a sharp nip of jealousy. And then Eithne, one of the musicians, was beside her. "We had such a good day. Yes, a good day. No gavvers. The workers were astonished, and then—how do you say it? Transformed. Yes, transformed."

"That's wonderful," Letta said, wishing she could have seen it.

Finn clapped his hands for silence. "And now," he said, "we celebrate."

The party went on all night. After eating, Finn retold the story of their adventure, praising Eithne and the other musicians. He held his glass aloft and made a toast. "To absent friends," he said. "To all those who went out and didn't come back. To those who chose to die so that others might be free. What we do today is for them. Our brothers. Our sisters. *Salut!*"

He raised his cup to the line of portraits, and everyone drank. Eithne and some of the other musicians started to play. Letta gave herself up to the sweet music and watched the dancers sway in the half-light. Before long, everyone was dancing. Letta hung back, suddenly shy. On the floor, she saw Marlo and Carmina, Carmina moving easily, her body fluid, Marlo following her as though they were one person. A little while later, the musicians stopped for a break, and Marlo and Carmina came to join her.

"Are you having a good time, Letta?" Marlo asked, his eyes soft and full of kindness.

Letta nodded. "Of course," she lied.

"You don't dance?" Carmina said.

Letta flushed. "No," she said. "I don't dance."

She didn't want to explain to Carmina that until a year ago she had never even heard music.

Carmina shrugged and held her hand out to Marlo. "Come on!" she said. "They're playing our tune."

Marlo hesitated. "You're sure you won't join us, Letta?" he asked.

"You go. I'm happy here."

Inside, she hoped he wouldn't go. She hoped he would stay with her. She chided herself even as that thought came. He didn't owe her anything. And he and Carmina had been friends for a long time. And yet… Letta felt a tingle every time he was near. Marlo shrugged and took Carmina's hand. They walked away from Letta, and the music swelled to a crescendo as all the instruments joined in.

She didn't care, she told herself, but she knew that wasn't true.

CHAPTER 3

#55

BANNED

NOT ALLOWED, AGAINST THE LAW

At breakfast the next day, Marlo pulled Letta aside. "There's a meeting tonight in Ark," he said. "In a safe house. Finn would like you to come."

Letta was startled. Finn had been adamant that she shouldn't leave the pump house other than to go to the hedge school.

"What's happening?" she said.

"You know that Finn has recruited a lot of volunteers in recent months? They've been divided into separate cells. That way, there's less chance of informers betraying us. Each cell has its own responsibilities, but they know nothing about what goes on in other cells."

Letta nodded. She had heard Finn talk about this system before.

"The cell we're visiting tonight is in charge of education. We need more schools. This cell wants to recruit more teachers. The more teachers we have, the more children we can reach. Finn thinks you should attend."

Letta felt her heart lift. She was thrilled that Finn trusted her with such important work. It was a small role, but it was something.

"We need to develop a plan," Marlo said. "We already know of two or three people we can trust to act as teachers. The more teachers we have, the more children we can reach."

"That's great," Letta said. "But we have to impress on them that they need to be cautious. The children need to be taught how to conceal the words as much as how to use them."

"And we need safe venues for the classes," Marlo said.

Letta nodded. Her thoughts were flying. "I'll work on it today," she said. "I'll prepare word cards and make a copy of the syllabus."

Marlo smiled. "It's good to see you excited again," he said. "These are great times, Letta. Things are starting to happen. It will take time, but we're going to win. I can feel it."

After he'd gone, Letta sat at her desk and thought about what he'd said. Could they really win? Letta tried to imagine Ark without its crippling laws. She tried to imagine a society that could say whatever it liked, think whatever it wanted to. A society that cherished music and art. It sounded like a utopia, but that had once been the way people really lived. Before the Melting. But then humans had ignored the danger of global warming, had not cherished the planet and had talked themselves into believing whatever suited them. Could they do better this time? Could they use words responsibly? She hoped so. And she wanted to play her part. She wanted to be one of the people who changed Ark. She would use her talents any way she could to achieve that.

Letta spent the day working on her plan. She drew up a list of words that the children would learn. She drew up codes of behavior to ensure good security. By evening, her eyes were tired, but her heart felt lighter.

They left the pump house as soon as darkness fell, Finn, Marlo, and Letta. The men wore big coats and cloth caps pulled down over their eyes. Letta had covered her clothes with a black shawl that also managed to cover her glowing red hair. Carmina had put charcoal streaks on their faces so they looked like people who were homeless. Even so, they knew their mission was a dangerous one.

Finn led them through the dark trees and down into the town. Since the battle at the Water Tower, they could no longer go through the gates of Ark. But the Creators had discovered new ways, dark alleys and safe houses, ways to enter Ark without the scrutiny of the gavvers.

Letta followed Finn as he negotiated these new routes. They approached the Tin Town end of the wall, and Finn deftly removed four large stones. He stood back as Letta and Marlo squeezed through the gap and then followed them before carefully replacing the stones. Then they scurried down an alleyway. At the corner, Finn stopped. Letta saw him look up and down before signaling to them to follow.

Letta tried to take in the town as they moved through it, remembering it as it had been a year ago and seeing it now, worn down and exhausted-looking. Many of the windows were boarded up; the paint on the walls of the houses was chipped and peeling. Amelia spent no time on the niceties. The place had never been beautiful, but now it was grim and seemed to warn interlopers that they would find no friendship here.

They were at the far end of the town from Letta's home. The tanner's shop was still there, the sickly smell of rotting hides hanging on the air, just as it had a year earlier. Five houses down, Finn stopped. He gave three sharp knocks on the wooden door. A young woman opened it. She was slender with short black hair and sharp eyes. She glanced up and down the street before hurrying them inside.

"No harm!" Marlo said when they were inside the house.

The girl smiled. "This way," she said and led them down the dark hallway to the room at the far end. The room was stark and clean, designed by the Green Warriors to shelter people but not to indulge them. The walls were an industrial gray; the one small window was shuttered. There was a plain metal table and four chairs. The only light was from a cluster of candles because there was no electricity in Ark once the working day was over.

Letta counted five people—two men and three women. She didn't recognize any of them. The girl who had ushered them in introduced herself as Marta. The two men were brothers, Carl and Vincent. Carl was much younger than his brother, not much older than Letta. He had curly brown hair and dark-brown eyes. He had a gap between his front teeth when he smiled. She thought he had the kind of face that was used to smiling. Nobody offered a last name, and Finn introduced Letta and Marlo only by their first names. The three women eyed them keenly but said nothing.

As soon as they were all seated, Vincent, a tall, good-looking man with a shock of coal-black hair, turned to Finn. "Thank you, Finn. Good you come."

"You are welcome, Vincent. Thank you for having us."

"We want teach children," he said, his face contorted with effort as he struggled to find the words he needed.

"Of course," Finn said. "We have to help the children, or they will become wordless."

"Babies now taken," Marta said. "You hear that?"

"I've heard rumors," Finn said carefully. "It may be just talk."

"Mothers frightened," Marta insisted. "Babies taken."

"Is there a mother we can talk to?" Finn said. "A mother who lost a baby?"

Marta shook her head.

"No talk," she said. "Afraid."

Finn sighed.

"I will look into it, Marta," he said. "But tonight we are here to talk about the hedge schools."

"Hedge school good," Vincent said with a slight smile, and he did a mock bow in Letta's direction.

"We need more of them," Marlo said.

One of the other women stood up. She was small, and her gray, pinched face was devoid of expression.

"How we help?" she said. "How?"

Letta wanted to tell them that they need not speak List, but she had seen it many times before. People became institutionalized. They were used to List. It would take time for them to relax enough to speak any other way.

"Letta," Finn said. "You have some thoughts about this?"

All the eyes in the room turned to her.

"Yes," she began, feeling shy. "I have made a curriculum."

"A what?" The small woman sounded annoyed.

"Sorry," Letta said. "I mean a—"

"Hush!" Vincent was standing at the window. No one moved. "There's something happening on the street."

Letta heard it then. Raised voices and a scuffle of some sort. An angry battering on the front door filled the room.

"Carl River! We know you there. Open up. Gavvers!"

Letta watched Carl freeze, his eyes wide.

"You'd best go through the back door," Vincent said in a tight whisper. "Quickly now."

Letta followed Marlo through to a dark corridor, and they edged forward until they came to the back door. Carl stayed close to them. He opened the door a crack and looked out. Then he closed it silently. "House surrounded," he hissed. "Go upstairs. All way to attic."

They slipped up the back stairs like ghosts. The stairs creaked in protest, and Letta wondered if the gavvers could hear it in the street. At the top was a short ladder. One after the other, they climbed it and dragged themselves into the room above: Marlo, Finn, Letta, and finally Carl.

There was barely room for the four of them. They stood huddled together, hardly daring to breathe, as Carl pulled up the ladder and closed the door in the floor. Letta stood shoulder to shoulder with him, so close that she could feel the heat radiating from his body. She couldn't see his face in the inky darkness of the attic, but she could hear his strangled breath and almost smell his fear.

They heard the door open downstairs. Raised voices. A thump. Letta imagined a body falling. She flinched. She heard a door closing. Then footsteps on the stairs. Carl creaked the trapdoor open.

Vincent looked up at them. "Quick," he said. "They gone but no trust. Come back. Want Carl."

"The gavver named Carver?" asked Finn.

Vincent nodded. "Carver. Others too, but Carver boss."

Letta knew Carver. An image of the gavver flashed

before her as she climbed down the ladder. Shaved head, meaty hands, bulbous nose.

"Let's go," Finn said, when they were all back in the hall.

Letta glanced at Carl. He looked frightened. She pulled Finn aside. "Shouldn't we take him with us? They'll come back for him. You heard his brother."

Finn hesitated.

"Please, Finn. Don't leave him here. We can't leave him behind." Without waiting for Finn to respond, she turned to the young man. "Carl," she said. "You come with us. It's not safe for you here."

Carl nodded, though he seemed reluctant. "Go where?"

Finn caught Carl's arm. "Don't ask any questions," he said. "Just come."

Carl turned to his brother. "I be back soon."

Vincent embraced him. "Go safe," he said.

The door opened, and they were back on the street. The journey home was dark and tense. The streets were quiet, but that only made Letta more nervous. At every corner she wondered if Carver and his men were there, ready to pounce. They made their way to where they had breached the wall and from there out into the forest. The moon floated above them, lighting the way, and in time the great pump house loomed out of the dark.

Once inside, Letta and the others were quiet, listening for any sound from the gavvers.

Carmina suddenly appeared and confronted Carl. "Who are you?" she said, and Letta could almost see her hackles rising.

"This is Carl," Letta said. "He's a friend. We had a run-in with some gavvers."

"Is he staying here?"

Finn nodded.

"How do we know we can trust him?" Carmina persisted.

"He belongs to a cell in town that has been working on education. He was at a meeting with us when the gavvers came," Finn explained patiently.

"This was the meeting about the hedge schools?"

Finn nodded.

"It seems like a lot of risk just to teach people a few words. And now we've inherited this stray because of it."

Letta felt the blood rise in her cheeks. "I think it's more than a few words," she said. "These children will never be able to speak properly—they will never have a mother tongue—if we don't help them."

Carmina scowled. "All I'm saying is that there will be time for all that after the revolution. This is a time to fight, not a time for childish things."

"Childish things?" Letta said. "You think that is what this is about? You think John Noa banned language because it is a weak, childish thing? You still have language, Carmina, but many others do not. It's easy for you to see words as having no value."

Carmina said nothing.

Letta plowed on. "Language is a weapon," she said. "And right now, that weapon has been taken from our people. You may know about soldiering, Carmina, but you know nothing about Ark if you can't see that."

Carmina looked as though Letta had slapped her. She opened her mouth to respond, but Marlo got there before her.

"That's enough. Now is not the time for argument. Let's all sit down and have some tea."

"Marlo is right," Finn said. "Now is not the time. Come, Carl. Let's get you a drink."

Carmina shrugged, her pretty face dark as thunder. "As you wish," she said and stalked back to her own living quarters.

CHAPTER 4

67

SCHOOL

PLACE TO LEARN WORDS

Carl fit into the pump-house family without a ripple. He was a quiet young man given to long periods of silence, and when he did speak, it was always in a hushed, respectful tone. He was about three years older than Letta but seemed far more world-weary. The gavvers were still looking for him. The Creators' sources had told them he was wanted for crimes of a subversive nature, but Letta knew no more than that. She was just glad she had persuaded Finn to rescue him.

Carl had worked as a baker in Ark, and Letta was delighted when he was put with her on cooking duty. They were making a rabbit stew. The rabbits had been found on the road quite dead, and the foragers had collected a selection of vegetables to cook with them. Letta's nose was full of the scent of dried rosemary and garlic as the pot bubbled on the stove.

"There are some apples in box in back hall," Carl said. "We cook them with honey if you like?"

Letta smiled. "You're good at this. I'm not able to cook."

"You never had to. Not your fault." He still spoke mostly List, but Letta noticed that he was slowly returning to normal language. It would take time.

"I have to go shortly, Carl. I have a class."

"I come?" He looked at her hopefully.

"I don't know," she said. "Marlo normally comes with me." She saw the disappointment in his eyes. "Why don't you ask Finn?"

"I will," he said. "I'd like to help."

And with that, he left. Letta finished cooking the meal and set it aside. They would reheat it in the evening.

Carl came in smiling as she finished up. "I'm to go with you and Marlo," he said. "I learn."

"I will learn." Letta corrected him automatically, then covered her mouth with her hand, embarrassed. "I'm sorry. I'm so used to correcting the children."

"No, please," Carl protested. "Do correct me. I want to learn."

"That's something I still dream about," Letta said.

"What is?" Carl's voice was gentle.

"School. Learning. You know, before the Melting all children went to school, and many of them went to universities where they did nothing but learn. Benjamin told me all about it. I would love that. I like teaching, but I don't know enough. I want to read books with thousands of words. I want to hear arguments and find out how other people think. Sometimes I feel that my world is so small."

"Me too," Carl said. "This is not world I would choose to live in. But have no choice. It is what it is."

"If we weren't in Ark, what would you like to do, Carl?"

He shrugged. "I don't care. I just want place where safe. Where family safe. That's all."

"Do you have many family in Ark?"

"Not so many. We lost my mother, but my father here, my brother, two sisters, a nephew, and a niece."

"You are lucky," Letta said.

"Maybe," Carl said. "More you have, though, more that can be taken away."

There was a catch in his voice, as if emotion might overwhelm him. She reminded herself, not for the first time, that it was dangerous to ask too many questions.

Later, at the hedge school, Letta noticed how keenly Carl listened as she spoke to the children. Marlo was on the knoll keeping guard, and the scholars were telling her their news from the town.

"My mam sad," Thaddeus offered after a while.

"Why is she sad?" Letta asked.

"Baby gone." The little boy's face crumpled, and fat tears rolled down his cheeks.

"It's all right, Thaddeus," his brother Aaron said. "Don't cry."

Letta looked at Aaron. "What baby?" she said.

"People in house next door. Had small baby. Thaddeus like. Then baby gone."

"Did it die?" Letta asked.

Aaron shrugged. "Don't know. Parents say nothing."

Letta said no more, but inside her mind was racing. This was what Marta had been talking about. But children were precious in Ark. What had happened to the child? If it had died, surely people would know! She looked at Carl and he shrugged, looking as puzzled as she felt. She drew her mind back to the lesson.

"Remember what I said the last time. We should choose our words carefully. Before the Melting, people threw words around as though they had no value. When we say something, we should mean it. Our words should be our bond. Truth should be our goal. That is just as important as knowing what an adjective is!" She laughed then. "Not that we don't need adjectives. Do you remember what an adjective is, my Thaddeus?"

Thaddeus smiled, his early distress forgotten. "A 'scribing word," he said confidently.

Letta clapped her hands. "Yes!" she said. "Clever boy! A describing word."

On her way back to the pump house, Letta told Marlo

what Thaddeus had said about the baby. He was as mystified as she was.

"Marta was convinced that babies were being taken. Remember? She spoke to Finn."

"Finn thought it might only be gossip," Marlo said.

"Will he follow up on it?"

Marlo shook his head. "Finn has other things to worry about at the moment," he said.

Letta looked at him and raised an eyebrow. "Something going on?" she said.

"Finn has big plans," Marlo said. "Change is finally coming."

Letta felt her heart quicken. "Really? Tell me more."

"It's not mine to tell," Marlo said. "Finn will tell everything when the time is right."

"Is there going to be trouble?" Carl's voice sounded strained, Letta thought.

"You could say that," Marlo said and grinned.

Letta had to wait till late that evening to get Marlo on his own. "What's happening?" she said.

"Finn has a plan to shake things up," Marlo said. "Tomorrow I'm going to do a reconnaissance. I need to go to the gavvers' base and get the lay of the land. There's a young gavver working on the desk who likes illegal alcohol. We may be able to turn him."

"Turn him?"

"Make him work for us."

"You mean blackmail him?" Letta said.

"We are at war, Letta," Marlo said. "We do things that you wouldn't do in peacetime."

Letta thought about what he'd said. She still didn't like it. And yet she agreed with Marlo. They would have to do hard things if they were going to change their world. Words might not be enough. And she was worried for Marlo. What if the gavvers recognized him? What if they arrested him? She still had nightmares about the time Benjamin spent in a cell. He had been tortured. She had seen the results. Her mind flashed back to his deathbed and the bloodied fingernails, evidence of all he had endured. The thought of Benjamin made her harden her heart. If the gavver could help them, they should get his help even if the cost was high.

The pump house had a strange atmosphere that evening. There was tension but also excitement. She watched Finn talking to Carmina, talking to the scouts, planning, explaining, doing what he did best. She kept her head down, writing words, preparing lessons. She was still baffled by the story about the missing babies. She had talked to Mrs. Pepper who used to work in Central Kitchen about it.

"It's not the first I've heard of," Mrs. Pepper said.

"There was at least one other case a few weeks ago. A baby was seen in the tanner's house. Belonged to young Gustav. Now there is no word of it. It's as if the family is denying it ever existed."

"Why would anyone want those babies?"

"Not anyone," Mrs. Pepper said. "Gavvers."

"You think the gavvers had something to do with it?"

"I know they did," Mrs. Pepper said. "I was talking to Gustav's mother at a meeting last week. She was never a woman to hold her tongue. When I asked her whether something had happened to the child, she said I'd have to ask a gavver to get an answer to that question. When I pushed her, she looked terrified and wouldn't say any more."

"Have you told Finn?"

Mrs. Pepper nodded. "I mentioned it to him, but he has too much on his mind, poor man. He can't go chasing shadows."

Letta's mind was racing. Why would the gavvers take children from their parents? Were they planning to use them to control the adults? Something shifted in her head. Finn didn't have time to chase shadows, but she did.

She was going to talk to Gustav's mother. Her heart quickened at the thought. This was something that she could do. Something important. She could talk to Gustav's mother and find out what was happening. The thought crystallized in her head. She had to go back to Ark.

Werber watched as Carver walked away from him down the corridor toward the front door. He had found them. The rat's nest that they had been looking for since Noa died. The Desecrators. Carver had found them buried in the forest. They had used Carl River as their spy.

Werber remembered Carl River well. He had been in school with him. Carl was a few years older and always seemed very happy. A smiley boy, he thought. Always smiling.

He wasn't smiling now.

They had intercepted a letter he had written to his brother. Full of forbidden words and vicious intent. He had been in league with the Desecrators, working with Finn. A night in the cells had reminded him of the consequences of his treachery—not just for himself but for his beloved family. And now the trap was set.

Werber shrugged. He had no pity for Carl. He had been born into a family that loved him. In contrast, he, Werber, had been a third-born in a world where only two children were permissible. Another couple had taken him in. He never felt like he belonged with them and then the father died, leaving him with a mother drowning in self-pity. She was dead now too. He didn't care. Amelia was his family now, and he was one of the most powerful people in Ark. He wondered if his birth family realized that. They were still alive.

He was strangely excited. Would Letta be in the pump house? Should he ask that she be brought to him right away?

As he passed a darkened window, he checked his reflection. He brushed his hair back from his face and smiled. His teeth shone white as bone in the dim light.

CHAPTER 5

#45

ENEMY

NOT FRIEND, DANGEROUS

It was late afternoon by the time Letta got to speak to Marlo.

"You look flustered," Marlo said with a smile playing on his face as she approached him.

"No, not really," Letta said. "But I wanted to talk to you. I need to go into Ark."

Marlo shook his head, and Letta felt her excitement fade a little. "Finn would never agree to it, Letta. You know that. It's too dangerous. The gavvers are everywhere, watching, listening. Amelia is clamping down on anyone that raises their voice. Imagine how she feels about us."

Letta felt her shoulders sag. She had to convince him. "It's important, Marlo. Really important."

"Has something happened?"

She saw the concern etched in his eyes. Those beautiful

eyes that she had always loved. But she couldn't let herself be distracted by that now—she had to press on. "I feel…claustrophobic. I'd like to see my old home. One last time. Even if it's only from a distance."

It wasn't the truth, but it would have to do. She didn't want to tell him about the babies. Not yet. Not till she knew something solid.

She looked up at him. "Please, Marlo."

"I am sorry, Letta. I know you love that old place, but remember it's just a building. They can only hurt you with this if you let them."

The unease he so clearly felt shadowed his face, and she hated herself for putting him in this position, but she couldn't stop herself. "Please, Marlo," she said.

He glanced over his shoulder toward Finn's office. "I don't know, Letta. I'll think about it, but I really don't think it's a good idea. The gavvers will be watching the shop."

"We could go at night," Letta pressed him. "I only want to go as far as the hill. I'll be able to see the shop from there."

Marlo groaned. "Letta! It's not that easy. And it's not worth the risk. Honestly."

She knew what he was saying was reasonable, but it didn't change the terrible urgency she felt.

She sensed something shifting in her head. "I'll go myself then," she said.

Marlo sighed. "Stop it, Letta," he said. "You're behaving like a child."

"Really?" she snapped at him. "Is that what you think? How quickly you've forgotten."

"Forgotten?"

"Forgotten how I risked my life to save yours."

As soon as the words were said, she wanted to unsay them. He flinched as though she had slapped him. Color flooded his cheeks. "I'm sorry you feel like that, Letta. But it doesn't change my thinking. I can't put everyone's life in danger on a whim."

He turned and walked away.

Letta leaned against the wall, watching him go. Waves of guilt pounded her. She hated what she had done to him. She hated the way he had looked at her. But another part of her didn't care. She needed to do something. She needed to contribute to the fight, not just be a bystander. But what had felt like an exciting adventure now felt more like a betrayal, and there was nothing she could do about it.

She sat as far away from Marlo as she could at dinner-time. She was glad when Carl sat next to her.

"You look tired," he said, as they ate.

"I have a lot on my mind," Letta said.

"Anything I can help with?"

"Not really," she said. "I need to go down to Ark. There's something I have to do."

"Something important?"

"I think so," Letta said, keeping her voice low. Carmina was sitting opposite, and Letta had no wish to involve her in the conversation.

"Won't that be dangerous?" Carl said, chewing on the knuckle of his small finger. Letta had noticed he always did that when he was stressed.

"As dangerous as everything else we do," she said, going back to her meal.

"Do you want me to come with you?" Carl asked, looking at her intently.

Letta shook her head. "No. Thank you. I'm only going to my old home. I can manage."

"Good," Carl said. "When will you go?"

"I don't know," Letta said. "Maybe tomorrow. After dark."

Carl nodded and went back to his dinner. He didn't speak again for the rest of the meal.

All the next day, Letta avoided Marlo. She hadn't spoken to him since their argument. He was avoiding her, too; she was sure of that. For the first time she felt like an outsider. Benjamin used to say that all the wordsmiths who had gone before them were outsiders: people on the edge, watching and recording. Maybe that was her fate.

She had made up her mind. She would leave at nightfall. She knew where the tanner's house was. She would slip in and be back before anyone knew she had gone.

Night came swiftly. As darkness fell and people settled down to sleep, Letta climbed into bed with her clothes on.

By ten, everyone else was asleep, and a deep hush filled the building. Letta grabbed her satchel and climbed the wooden stairs to the trapdoor in the ceiling. She opened it carefully. In the hallway, Josh, one of the guards, was waiting. He was on sentry duty inside. There would be two more guards outside. Josh nodded at Letta. "What's happening, Letta?" he said.

"I have to run an errand for Finn," she answered.

Josh frowned. "At this hour?"

"The only hour I can do it, I'm afraid," Letta said. "Don't worry. Finn has everything arranged."

Josh looked perplexed. "He didn't mention it," he said.

"Security," Letta said, the story she had rehearsed slipping easily from her mouth. "I'll be back soon."

She waited as Josh checked that it was safe for her to leave.

Despite the tension she was feeling, Letta was stunned by the beauty of the night. The trees were washed silver by the cold light from the moon, and all around small animals rustled in the undergrowth. She looked up at the moon and remembered how as a child she had loved it. How many nights had she stood at her bedroom window looking up at its gnarled white face? In the time before the Melting, man had walked on the moon. Benjamin had told her that. They had walked on the moon and built a village of sorts on Mars. Maybe they knew that the day would come when they could no longer live on Earth. If that was the case, they had left it all too late.

She walked along the forest path lost in thought.

She wanted to talk to Marlo, to apologize, but she needed to talk to Gustav's mother first, and she couldn't risk Marlo dissuading her. She would talk to him afterward. Explain to him what she was trying to do. He would be proud of her.

Soon, the statue of the Goddess loomed out of the darkness above Letta. Her serene face was clear in the moonlight. She was cut from a single block of white marble. She had been there forever. Since before the Melting. They said she was the last prophetess who had come to warn the people that the end was nigh. They hadn't listened. Now she looked down on Letta like an apprehensive mother.

From the top of the hill, Letta had a clear view of Ark. The houses huddled together, the narrow streets, the tree-lined square. Somewhere in the distance a dog barked, and Letta thought she heard something rustle in the bushes behind her. She turned quickly, but there was nothing there. *Just my imagination*, she told herself, but at that moment she felt the hair on the back of her neck stand up, and her body shivered involuntarily. She looked around again. Nothing.

She made her way to the wall and removed the stones as

she had seen Finn do. It was harder work than she had imagined. The stones were heavy and awkward, but she persevered and managed to get in without any major trouble.

The town was quiet. Totally still.

Letta put her hand in her pocket and pulled out the old key that would unlock the back door of the shop. She had decided to take it with her at the last minute. She couldn't resist the chance to be back in the shop one last time. Surely the gavvers had more to do than watch her old home in the middle of the night? She would be in and out in a matter of minutes, and then she would visit the tanner's house.

She hurried along the street toward the wordsmith's shop. Every door and every window was closed. The only sound was the gentle hum of the windmills. Nothing moved. The moon was still bright in the sky, offering her no shadow to hide in. After what seemed like an eternity, she reached the mouth of the lane that ran along the side of the shop. She hurried on, happy to be off the main street. At the end of the lane, she turned left and found herself at the back door.

She took the key from her pocket and turned it in the lock. The door opened slowly, revealing the hallway beyond it, dark and bedecked with shadows. She didn't dare light the lamps. She made her way down the corridor behind the shop. Into the master's library. She stopped and inhaled the familiar smell. Old paper, dust, and Benjamin. She could feel his spirit here, a soft warmth. She went to his desk and picked up a single word card written in the old man's hand. *Hope.* As her hand touched the card, she froze. Was that a noise? She listened, not daring to breathe. Nothing.

Letta took a deep breath. Something was holding her back. Was there nothing more she could take with her? The source material? How could she leave it after all the work Benjamin had done to retrieve it? She would have to. She didn't think it would fit in her satchel, and it would be too awkward to carry. She sighed and pulled herself away, comforted by the feel of the card in her hand. She crossed the floor swiftly and heard the door close behind her with a hollow sigh. She hurried along the corridor toward the back door, her footsteps echoing in the empty house.

Passing the old oak door that led from the living area into the shop, she faltered. It stood ajar as if pleading with her to go in. She leaned against the warmth of its timber and could just see the cubbyholes through the gap between door and frame. The thought of her little boxes full of words almost destroyed her resolve, but she knew she couldn't loiter. She had to go to see the tanner's wife. She turned and headed for the street with a lump in her throat.

As she reached out to open the door, she saw something move out of the corner of her eye, and even before the scream left her throat, a gavver slipped out from the shadows. In horror, Letta saw that it was her old enemy, Carver. And worse than that, far worse, he had one arm around a young man's throat.

Letta's gaze fell on the familiar face. The high cheekbones. The blue-gray eyes. Marlo!

How could this be? Had he followed her? She hadn't imagined it. She had heard something. Her thoughts were thundering around, making no sense. She heard Marlo gasp, a tiny involuntary sound but a sound that tore at her heart.

Carver threw Marlo against the wall, then held him there with one hand. Slowly, he turned his head toward Letta.

"Wordsmith," he said. "Good, very good."

NON-LIST

SPY

A SECRET WATCHER

As if in slow motion, Letta saw Carver pull back his fist and hit Marlo in the face, then throw him across the floor. Marlo tried to save himself but twisted his ankle as he fell. He struggled to stand up, but Carver punched him again. Grasping him by the hair, Carver slammed him against the wall.

No! her brain screamed, but her body remained motionless. She forced the words out. "Stop!" she cried. "Please. Stop! It's me you want. Leave him alone."

Carver drove his elbow into Marlo's throat and rested there like a man leaning against a tree on a hot day. Marlo cried out and then fell quiet, though his arms continued to twitch. Letta tried to look away from him but couldn't.

She grabbed Carver's arm, rage simmering inside her. "Stop! You're hurting him," she said, but the man batted her away as though she were a fly. Letta came straight back at him, her hands clawing at his arm. "Stop it!" she said again.

Carver hit her with the back of his hand and sent her skidding along the floor. She lost her balance and fell, coming down heavily on her hip. She cried out in pain.

Carver looked at her blankly, then put more pressure on Marlo's throat. The boy groaned. A deep, animal sound.

Quickly, in one deft movement, Carver switched his grip and grabbed Marlo by the collar of his shirt and, with infinite ease, smacked the boy's head against the wall behind him. Once, twice, as though trying to crack a nut.

"You think you so smart," Carver said. "How you like new friend? How you like Carl?"

Letta tried to process what he was saying. What had it to do with Carl? She had told Carl. She had told him the plan. *No!* But the gavver was still talking, confirming the nightmare.

"He tell us everything. All about your school. Your big plans. Not so smart now."

At that precise moment, Marlo managed to get his knee free and thrust it into the other man's groin. Carver screamed and reached for his gun. In his haste, the weapon fell, clattering on the hard floor.

Now! Letta thought. She dropped the card still clutched in her fist, reached down, and managed to get her hand to the cold metal. Carver's boot stamped down on her fingers. Pain shot into her hand and up her arm, but she managed to grab the gun and hold on to it. She hefted it from the floor and pointed it at the man. "Get back!" she screamed, the gun heavy in her hands.

Carver looked at her and smiled. "Go on!" he said. "Shoot! Shoot, little girl!"

Letta noticed that her hand was trembling. She tried to steady it but she couldn't. Something beyond her control plucked at her arm, making the gun jump.

You have to shoot him, the voice in her head said. *It's only a Black Angel. A bullet that hurts and heals at the same time. He'll recover like Marlo did the time you first met him.* And she *wanted* to shoot him. She wanted to see him suffer.

But her heart told her she couldn't do it. There had to be another way.

Carver leered at her. "Can't pull trigger, can you?"

Letta felt all the heat leave her body. Beside her, Marlo moaned, but Letta couldn't bear to look at him. They had to get out of there. Carver was still standing in front of the door, blocking their escape route.

"Get out of my way!" she said, but the man only laughed.

"Wordsmiths! What use you to Ark? We burn this place. We burn it to ground! Now your friends at pump house see we know everything that goes on in Ark."

Then, like a snake, he sprang, a long, thin knife suddenly in his hand, and at that moment, Letta pulled the trigger.

Bang!

He fell. Blood spurted in a red, misty spray, covering Letta's hand and causing the gun to slip from her fingers. The blood continued to pump. She looked at the man, aghast. Gray-faced, eyes open, staring. The wound in his chest gaped, red and raw.

"Come on!" Marlo screamed at her, but she was transfixed. Words tumbled and dived through the air, screaming, calling.

Blood! Wound!

"We have to help him," she said. "Stop the bleeding!" She fell to her knees and thrust her hand into Carver's open chest, but the blood continued to spurt. Then, as suddenly as it had begun, it stopped. Letta looked up at Marlo. "Is he okay?" she asked.

She thrust her fingers into the soft flesh under the man's chin and felt for a pulse. Nothing.

"He's dead, Letta," Marlo said.

Letta stared at him, uncomprehending, blood dripping from her hands. "Dead? How can he be dead? A Black Angel doesn't kill."

Dead, deceased, departed.

The words were back like fireflies drawn to the flame. She had to ignore them. Listen to Marlo.

"It wasn't a Black Angel."

At that moment, someone hammered on the back door.

"Letta!" Marlo said. "Come on—move!"

"No!" Letta managed to spit the word out. "The card."

The card lay on the floor where it had fallen, with Carver's arm thrown on top of it. Letta snatched it up and watched as the gavver's hand flopped lifelessly back onto the floor.

"He can't be dead. A Black Angel doesn't kill," she whispered. "A Black Angel doesn't kill."

"Letta, please! Come! We have to warn the others. Through the front. Come on."

Letta followed him through the door into the shop, past the boxes of words. She stood transfixed as Marlo wrestled with the heavy bolt.

Then they were on the street and running.

CHAPTER 7

#74

DARK

TIME AFTER SUNSET, NO LIGHT

They ran toward the west, through the streets, taking every back alley Marlo knew. Letta looked back every few minutes but couldn't see anyone following them. Marlo moved stealthily, like a cat with perfect balance. Letta stumbled along, her breath burning her lungs, the stitch in her side holding her back. They turned the corner onto Fox Road. Letta saw something move in the shadows. She tugged on Marlo's arm, warning him to be quiet. She pointed.

Finn stumbled through first, blood pouring down his face, his body stooped at an unnatural angle. A gavver wielding a large club followed. Behind him came a line of men and women, their hands tied behind their backs, staggering into the dark night. They were strangely quiet. *Carl*, Letta thought desperately. Carl had betrayed them, just as Carver said. As she watched, she became aware of every detail. The scratching of their shoes on the cobbles, the way the wind tossed their hair, ever so gently, the anxious chatter of a nightingale. At least ten gavvers were with the group, big men, pushing and shoving. Violence emanated from them like a bad smell.

At the end of the line came Carmina. Letta heard Marlo take a sharp breath. Like the others, Carmina's hands were bound behind her back. As they watched, a gavver pushed her and she stumbled, then just as quickly lashed out with her foot, catching the man on the ankle. He let out a roar of pain, shattering the dark silence as he clutched the injured ankle with both hands. The procession stopped. Every head turned toward the noise. Letta heard Marlo suck in his breath.

"No!" he said in a hoarse whisper. "No!"

Letta took his hand and squeezed it. She didn't want to look. She didn't want to see what would happen to Carmina, but she couldn't look away either. Carmina threw back her head and laughed.

With that, a second gavver hit her on the back of the head with the butt of his gun. The girl dropped to the ground like a bird that had been shot from the sky. Finn tried to get to her, but one of the gavvers lunged at him, sending him sprawling on the dark cobbles too.

The man with the injured ankle stood looking down at Carmina's motionless body. Then, with his good foot, he kicked her in the ribs. Letta thought they were going to leave her there, but as the group started to move again, a gavver said something to Finn, who stood up and lifted Carmina, holding her in his arms as though she were a baby.

As soon as the last gavver disappeared around the corner, Letta turned to Marlo. "We have to get out of here," she said.

Marlo turned away from her. "No," he said. "I need to go after them. I have to find a way to rescue them."

Letta grabbed his arm, turning him toward her. "No, Marlo!" she said. "You can't help them. You'll end up in prison with them, and what good would that do?"

"I don't care," he said, pulling his arm away. "I can't just leave them."

Letta felt a knife pierce her heart. If she hadn't murdered Carver, they wouldn't be in this mess. They could stay and try to help Finn and the others. But they were fugitives now. They couldn't stay in Ark a minute longer. She looked straight into Marlo's eyes. "You have to listen to me," she said.

Marlo hesitated. She could see the yearning in his face. He wanted to follow them.

"We can't stay here, Marlo," she said gently. "Not now."

"And where can we go?" he said. "Where?"

Her mind raced. Where could they go? Where would they find shelter, water? Suddenly, they heard dogs barking in the distance. Gavvers. Letta knew it wouldn't take long for the dogs to track them down.

She knew where to go. The only place she knew outside

of Ark. Her only friend outside of Ark. Edgeware. Edgeware who had rescued Benjamin and kept him safe when he was banished. Maybe she could do the same for them?

"Come on!" she told Marlo. "Follow me."

Without another word, Marlo turned and went with her.

She had to get to the forest. Her heart beat a little faster. It was dangerous, but it was a place they could go. It was something. She caught Marlo's hand and started to run, the other hand still clutching the small white card.

CHAPTER 8

#81

RUN

MOVE FAST USING FEET

The musty dampness of the forest soaked into her bones. Thornbushes arched out of the undergrowth, their long arms clawing at her skin. She walked on.

There was a strange atmosphere in the forest as the sky began to lighten. It was a place cloaked in mystery and full of dread. No one was sure what was in there among the trees, but rumors abounded. Criminals fleeing the gavvers, ghosts of people long dead, and wild animals wandering at will.

Letta's mind kept returning to the last few hours, overrun with images of Carver lying on the floor, blood oozing from his chest, her own heart pounding, her knees shaking. She had murdered a man. Not just any man. She had murdered a gavver. For a second, she thought she would faint. She stopped and leaned on a tree, feeling its rough, wrinkled skin beneath her hand. *Keep walking! Keep walking!* The voice in her head would not be sated. She needed to think about something else. She would think about putting one foot in front of the other. One foot, then the other.

They had been walking in silence for over an hour. Letta found herself stopping every few minutes. Stopping to look around and see if she could remember a particular tree or a slight incline. After a few more grueling minutes, she stopped to rest.

"Sorry," she said to Marlo. "I need a break."

"We have to keep moving." Marlo's voice was flat.

Letta shrugged and looked at her feet, not wanting to meet his eyes. "Do you think we are going in the right direction?"

He nodded.

Neither of them spoke. In the distance, Letta heard an animal roar. A cat?

She shivered. She glanced at Marlo and saw him wipe a tear from his cheek. Letta didn't know what to say to him, how to comfort him. It was all her fault. Her fault that he was here, her fault that the others had been captured. She was the one who had insisted that they take Carl back to the pump house. She had destroyed everything that Finn and the others had built. How had she gotten it so wrong? Her mouth suddenly felt bone dry.

"I'm thirsty," she managed to say.

"I have a small bottle of water."

Water. What would they do in the forest without water?

"When we get to Edgeware's, we can rest," Marlo said. "Let's keep on for now."

He glanced behind him anxiously. Letta strained to hear if anyone was following them. The forest was eerily quiet. As they walked, Marlo pushed a branch away from him. It sprang back and lashed Letta's face, causing her to cry out. She put her hand to the welt and felt the warm dampness of her own blood.

"I'm sorry," Marlo said as he examined the damage.

Letta tried not to wince. She could smell the faint smell of wild sage, his smell. She tried to catch his eye, but he was concentrating on the wound. Would he ever be able to forgive her? She pulled away reluctantly and they continued on.

They walked on. An hour passed and then another. Letta saw something. A shape in the near distance. A house? She caught Marlo's arm. He stopped. Letta nodded in the direction of the building. As they got nearer, Letta could see that it was a shed. Someone had patched the holes in the wall, and they'd put on a roof with bits of old tin and slats of timber.

They moved closer. Letta could see the door now. She looked at Marlo. He nodded and she put her hand on the handle. As she opened the door, Letta caught the cloying smell of decay followed by a whiff of wild garlic. She groped with one hand, meeting cobwebs and dead flies as she cleared a path. The room inside felt cold and dank and grim as hunger. A rough table made from a flat rock sat in the center of the room and beside it a bench made from a hollow log. There was even a window of sorts. A square had been cut into the wall originally, and now it was filled with a piece of glass.

"Somebody has been here since the Melting," Letta said softly. She looked around.

There was a tin box on the floor. She opened it gingerly. Inside she found a cup, a spoon, and a plate along with a box of matches, a battered metal saucepan, and a hammer. Before she could show her find to Marlo, he had disappeared outside. He came back almost immediately.

"There's a small barrel of water outside. Clean water. One of those sealed barrels they use in Ark at the distribution sites. We won't die of thirst."

"I'll go look for something to make a hot drink with," she said, heading back outside.

In the undergrowth, she found plenty of nettles and some bindweed, and then she saw what she had come for. Wild burdock! Big, green heart-shaped leaves and spiky purple flowers, but Letta didn't want the leaves or the flowers. She needed the root. A quick survey produced a relatively flat stone, and Letta started to scrape away at the base of the plant.

She didn't see it till she felt something cold on the back of her hand, its body thick and fleshy, its pointed head protruding from its body, and two flintlike pouched eyes glaring up at her—a snake!

Then it all happened in seconds. She pulled her hand back. The snake reared, mouth open, fangs suddenly appearing. Letta knew it was about to pounce. She tightened her hold on the stone and smashed it down on the green head. A spurt of venom sprayed her arms. Letta raised the stone again, but the snake was faster. Once more she found herself staring at the sharp fangs. Once more the snake's mouth went for her. This time, Letta managed to sidestep it. With the last of her strength, she hit it with the stone, again and again. Finally, it stopped moving altogether.

Letta's knees buckled, and she dropped to the forest floor. Her heart was beating so hard it was deafening. She tried to breathe, to calm herself, but she couldn't take her eyes off the snake. Her hands hurt from clutching the stone, and suddenly she was back in the shop, her hand clutching the gun while Carver lay dying at her feet. Acid filled her mouth, and she thought she would get sick. She had taken three lives now. Three lives. Noa and Carver and now the snake. She couldn't imagine herself killing any living creature a year ago. What was happening to her? Slowly, she picked up the burdock root and headed back, never taking her eyes off the ground.

Marlo had made a small fire outside the hut.

"We can make soup," Letta said. Though she was still

shaken from her ordeal with the snake, she was determined to hide that from Marlo. "You haven't eaten since the pump house."

Marlo nodded, but she saw the dark cloud that passed over his face when she mentioned the pump house.

Letta placed the burdock root to simmer in boiling water in the old saucepan. They took turns drinking from the single cup, and by the time they were finished, the winter sun was high in the sky and dappled light fell all around them, lighting the forest floor and revealing the multitudes of insects that lived there.

As the afternoon wore on, Marlo collected nettles and wild garlic, along with a handful of mushrooms. Having heard Letta's story of the snake, he moved cautiously around the hut.

"Do you think they're okay?" Letta said as gently as she could when he came back with his harvest. "Finn and the others?"

"I hope so," Marlo said.

Letta could scarcely bear to look at him. His face was suffused with anguish—yes, *anguish*, that was the correct word.

Anguish: deep mental distress.

Letta sat looking at him, overcome with sympathy but with something else too. She struggled to identify the emotion, the thing that gave her an ache in her stomach and made her throat constrict. Guilt.

Marlo stood up. "I'll get some more firewood. We'll need it later."

Letta watched him go.

He was gone for hours, leaving Letta feeling anxious as she waited for him to return. Her thoughts were never far from the dead gavver. Did he have a family? Was there someone who had loved him? Why had there been live ammunition in the gun? John Noa wouldn't kill anything. Not directly. He threw people into the forest to be eaten by animals, but he wouldn't allow the gavvers to actually kill someone. He had invented the Black Angel. A bullet that wounded, then cauterized the veins and let the wound heal. It left a mark, a dark cloud, on the person's skin. It had never occurred to her that Amelia would change the rules.

Why had Letta gone back to Ark at all? Why had she thought that she could make a difference? If she had been content to obey Finn's orders, none of this would have happened. If she hadn't trusted Carl, the gavvers would never have found the pump house. If she hadn't baited Marlo, he wouldn't have followed her. The guilty thoughts chased round and round, making her feel ill.

She collected bracken and moss and made two beds in the hut. It took her hours because she kept stopping. Stopping to check for snakes. Stopping to see if Marlo was coming. Stopping to listen for gavvers.

As the evening drew in, she began to wonder if Marlo

would come back at all. Maybe he had planned that all along, to leave her alone in the forest and head back to Ark to try to rescue Finn and the others. She pushed the thought away, but the effort made her head feel hot and sore. She kept the fire lit and put the saucepan on to make fresh soup.

When Marlo came back, he brought six eggs stolen from a bird's nest.

"A pheasant, I think," he said, handing them to her very gently. "We can cook them in the soup."

Letta had opened her mouth to reply when she heard something. A roar. She looked in the direction of the noise. Marlo looked too. They strained hard to hear it again. Seconds later they heard another roar.

"A bear," Marlo said. "Take the saucepan and get inside."

Letta grabbed the saucepan while Marlo kicked over the fire, smothering the embers. As they went through the door of the shed, they heard it again, nearer this time. A growl. With shaking hands, she bolted the door. Marlo stood at the window looking out.

"It probably won't bother us," he said. "But we need to eat the food. Bears have an acute sense of smell, and we don't want anything to tempt him."

They cracked the eggs into the hot soup and had their meal. Then they cleaned out the pot and went back to the window to watch for the bear. The night was drawing in, and with it, the wind rose, whipping branches in a mad ballet. Letta shivered as it howled through the trees and sneaked in through the cracks in the shed.

Marlo put his arm around her shoulders. "I always think it sounds like the sea with the tide being pulled in, then thrown out again. Listen!"

Letta tried to relax and reimagine what she was hearing, but there was something so lonely about the wailing of the wind that she was almost relieved when the rain came. Its thundering on the wooden roof drowned out all other sounds.

"I thought you might not come back," she said. "This afternoon. I thought you might not come back."

He didn't say anything. Did that mean he had considered it? She looked up at him, but he was looking into the distance, his jaw taut.

"Do you think he's gone?" Letta asked, touching Marlo on the arm. He jumped, startled.

"The bear? Yes," he said and lapsed into silence.

An hour or so later, lying on her makeshift bed, Letta listened to Marlo sleep. She was reminded of those nights when he had stayed with her in the shop, when she first met him. She tried to relax, to let go of the horrors of the previous twenty-four hours. After a few minutes, she heard him tossing, shuddering, muttering to himself. She sat up, alarmed. Was he feverish again? Then she realized he was talking, and after a few seconds the words became clear.

"Carmina!" That's what he was saying. "Carmina."

Her heart plummeted. Would he ever forgive her? If something bad happened to Carmina, to Finn, how would they ever get over that? And what would her life be like without him? The thought of how much he meant to her worried her. She didn't want to be dependent on him. She had lost everyone she had ever really loved. Her parents and then Benjamin. And if Marlo loved Carmina, there would be no future for Letta with him.

Finally, she slept. In the morning, she woke to find him already awake and looking at her. "I'm sorry," she said, consumed with shyness. "I hope you got some sleep."

He leaned toward her, his mouth coming toward her mouth. Was he going to kiss her? Her heart thundered. She moved nearer to him.

"You have a cobweb there," he said, brushing her hair lightly. Her eyes widened. She had been so sure. He smiled, the blue-gray eyes twinkling. Could he read her thoughts? "Pity we don't have any more of that awful soup you made."

They both laughed, and Letta felt as though someone had taken away a huge weight that had held her down since she had shot Carver. She stood up to get a drink of water. As she walked across the floor, a flash of white caught her eye. She bent down and saw a card half-hidden by the log in the middle of the floor.

She picked it up. Her eyes scanned it, then widened in surprise. It was a word card written in her own hand. In Ark, every trade was allowed extra words to cover the work they did. A shoemaker might have *last* and *hammer*, a tanner *hide* and *skin*. She examined the card carefully.

> *Criminal: person guilty of crimes against Ark.*

"Gavvers," she said softly. "This is a word card for a gavver."

Werber looked up from the table. He had been about to eat his lunch. He put down the mug of water and focused on the gavver.

"She no go away," the man said. "She want talk you."

Outside, the wailing was still audible. Despite everything, he felt a pang of sympathy. He remembered how the cows on his uncle's farm used to cry when the calves were taken away.

"There is nothing I can do," he said, trying to keep his voice cold, emotionless. "Take her away. I cannot eat my lunch with that noise."

He went back to his food. He could hear the man hesitate. Please go, he thought. Please. He heard the gavver turn, and a few seconds later the door opened and closed.

Werber got up from the table. He had to be strong, he told himself, but he couldn't stop imagining the woman's pain. Her baby boy was only a few weeks old, and Werber's men had come and taken him. He knew her crying would haunt his dreams, but there was no other way.

Fifty babies now. Fifty bereft mothers. More responsibility heaped on his shoulders. He would see to it that the children were well cared for. He would go out into the countryside and inspect the farm where they were to be kept. He still remembered what it was like to be taken from his parents. Such was the lot of third children in Ark. One too many.

He sat down again and picked up his spoon, but he had lost his appetite. He hadn't agreed with the babies being taken from their mothers. He had tried to dissuade Amelia, but despite all his new words, he had failed. The babies were the future, Amelia said. They had to make sure they were not contaminated with language. The Green Warriors were confident that if the babies could be kept in isolation, they would never succumb. He had found it difficult to believe, but they had assured him. These children were important. They were the beginning and the end, they said. The beginning and the end.

CHAPTER 9

#227

HERB

PLANT, CAN EAT

"W e can't stay here," Marlo said, already starting to gather up their things. "If this is a gavvers' outpost, it's only a matter of time before they come here."

Letta looked at the card in her hand. Marlo was right. She picked up her satchel.

"Take the matches, and let's fill some bottles with water."

Letta moved mechanically. Gavvers could arrive at any moment. One of their own had been murdered. They wouldn't rest until they found the killer.

"We should head north," Marlo said.

"Let's go, then," said Letta. "We can gather some food here before we move on. There are more herbs over there where I found the burdock."

Her stomach was already grumbling, a dull ache that wouldn't go away.

She put her satchel over her shoulder and headed off, closely followed by Marlo. Within minutes, they were gathering the scant harvest of herbs that managed to grow in the shade of the forest—the lime-green nettles and tiny blue violets, along with young dandelions and sturdy chickweed.

They walked on, saying nothing. Letta was lost in her own thoughts. *If the gavvers find us…* She couldn't think like that. She had to believe they wouldn't find them. She clutched her satchel to her chest.

The trees were bearing down on her on every side. All her senses were on full alert. She felt eyes watching her from the undergrowth. She shook herself. She couldn't let her imagination run away. They walked on, picking their way among briars and rocks, watchful, waiting, never letting their guard down.

Finally, they gave in to exhaustion and sat under a tree to rest. Letta was still wrapped up in her own thoughts, but she tried to tune in to what Marlo was saying.

"How soon do you think we can go back to Ark?"

"I don't know," she said.

How could they ever go back? The whole mess was her fault. If she hadn't insisted on going to the shop, the gavver would be alive, and she and Marlo could have done something to help Finn.

"Carl was a spy," she said now. With all the stress of the last days she hadn't managed to process that.

"Yes," Marlo said. "He was."

Her mind went back to the night she had first met him. The night they had hidden in the attic. How easily they had escaped! The gavvers must have known those houses had attics, but they never searched the one in Carl's house. They *wanted* Carl to escape, to be taken in by the Creators. The cuckoo in the nest. *And I trusted him*, Letta thought. *I was so naive.*

"Don't judge him too harshly," Marlo said. "You don't know what they had on him."

Letta nodded, but inside she was seething. How could anybody do that? How could he betray the people who had given him shelter?

"I don't know if I can go back to Ark," she said now. "There is no role for me there. Amelia has won. It will take someone bigger and braver than I am to topple her."

"You can't just give up, Letta. You defeated Noa."

"Did I?" Letta looked up at him. "That was more by accident, I think. I'm only an ordinary person, Marlo. I can't change the whole world. I've had enough."

Even as the words left her mouth, she knew she meant it and that this was her new reality. Her future wasn't in Ark. Not anymore.

"I think you're tired," Marlo said. "And still in shock. You'll feel differently later."

He offered her his hand, and she took it, but in her heart she knew she wouldn't change her mind.

They walked on, both lost in their own thoughts. Then Letta felt Marlo stop. She looked up. A man was walking toward them.

He was tall as well as broad. In his hand he held a knife, casually, as though it were meant to be there at the end of his arm. He was dressed in what looked like animal hides sewn together with string, and where his arm was exposed, Letta could see the scars that crisscrossed his skin, ghostly white snakes. She looked at his face, with its weather-reddened skin and deep-set eyes. He looked back at her, equally curious. "Who are you?"

The eyes had narrowed, and Letta felt he was looking right through her. The knife was now pointing at them. "Letta," she said. "And this is Marlo."

"Who are you?" he said again.

"Refugees," Letta said, determined to hold his gaze. "From Ark."

"We are on the run," Marlo added softly.

The man's head swiveled. "Why?"

"A problem with a gavver," Marlo said.

"I see," the man said. "That could be it, or you could be spies."

"We're not spies," Marlo said. "We are Creators."

"So you say. Now walk!" He waved the knife toward a small road to their left.

Letta looked at Marlo. He shrugged, and together they headed down the road in front of the man.

CHAPTER 10

NON-LIST

REGRET

TO FEEL SORRY OR GUILTY FOR

After about an hour, they came to a clearing. There were two makeshift tents and the remnants of a fire.

"Home, sweet home," the man said. "Sit!"

They sat on the damp ground while the man restarted the fire.

"What do we call you?" Marlo asked.

"Joe," the man said. "It's not my name but you can use it."

Now that Letta had time to study him, she could see he was on the late side of forty. He didn't look healthy—his skin was mottled and the whites of his eyes were a dull yellow color. *Two tents*, she thought. *He's not alone.*

The fire was lit, and Letta was glad of its warmth. The atmosphere was damp but not terribly cold, and the fire was comforting. She watched the man busy himself around the camp. What did he want from them? The knife was now in his belt, but she knew it was too dangerous to challenge him.

Just as the sun was easing down in the sky and dark shadows had started to gather, a woman arrived. She was about the same age as the man and just as tall. Her skin was blue-black, and Letta noticed that the whites of her eyes were yellow like the man's.

"We have company," the man said.

"I see that," she answered.

The man pulled her aside and Letta watched them as they talked, heads close together. Every so often, they looked over at the captives, but Letta couldn't figure out what they thought.

After a while, they came back to the fire.

"You are from Ark?" the woman said.

Letta nodded.

"And where are you headed?"

"We're going to see a friend," Marlo said.

"Name?" the man said.

"Edgeware," Letta answered.

"A friend of Edgeware is our friend too," the woman said, offering her hand. Letta shook it. It felt rough and callused. "I'm Danu."

The man grinned. "You should have mentioned Edgeware at the start," he said. "I might have given you a warmer welcome. My name is Rua."

"Not Joe, then?" Marlo smiled and shook his hand.

"We really are Letta and Marlo," Letta said.

"You must be hungry," Danu said and threw the bag she had been carrying to the ground. "We are here to hunt. We can feed you."

Letta felt her stomach contract; her mouth salivated. She hadn't realized how hungry she was. The woman put her hand into the bag and pulled out a brace of pigeons tied together at the feet.

Within minutes, the birds were plucked, and Rua had constructed a spit from a whittled piece of wood. Letta could barely contain herself as the birds turned slowly over the flames, spitting fat into the fire and filling her head with the delicious smell of roasting meat.

"We have some water." Marlo offered his bottle to the hunters.

"No need," Rua said. "No shortage of water. There's a stream over there behind those trees."

Letta looked at Marlo. Were Rua and Danu drinking polluted water? The heavy and persistent rainfall after the Melting had caused the nitrogen used in farmland to soak into the rivers and lakes. Toxic algae had quickly taken hold, making the water undrinkable.

"Isn't that dirty?" Letta asked.

"What choice do we have?" Rua answered.

"Won't it make you sick?"

"We have decided to risk that," Danu said gently, and Letta knew the conversation was over.

Soon they were tucking into roast pigeon and potatoes baked in the fire.

"We grow them," Rua said. "Back where we live."

"You don't live here?" Marlo said.

Danu shook her head. "We live about three days' walking away, but we travel this far to hunt."

"Are there many of you?" Letta asked.

"A small community," Rua said. "People come and go."

"Anywhere is better than Ark," Danu said. "We started out in Tin Town, but we left before Noa was overturned. We have heard it's no better now. Maybe even worse?"

Marlo nodded. "In some ways," he said.

"You heard there was a gavver murdered? We met a man yesterday. He was fleeing from Ark and full of news."

Letta nodded, not trusting herself to speak.

"Amelia is hell-bent on retribution. Houses are being raided, people arrested, people banished. That's what we heard," Rua added.

For a minute, no one spoke. Letta pulled in closer to the fire.

"Had the man heard anything about the Creators who were taken?" Marlo asked, leaning in closer to Danu.

She shook her head. "No. Sorry," she said.

"We've heard other disturbing things," Rua said. "Things even worse than raids and arrests."

Letta looked at him.

"Babies have been disappearing," he said. "Taken by the gavvers."

"Why?" Marlo asked. "What could they want with infants?"

Rua shrugged. "We don't know," he said. "The gavvers have warned the parents to keep their mouths closed or worse will befall them."

Danu shook her head. "It isn't natural to separate a child from its mother like that. No good will come of it."

"We heard something about it before we left," Letta said. "A little boy I was teaching mentioned that a child had gone missing."

"What did you do in Ark?" Danu said, looking at her with curiosity.

"I was the wordsmith's apprentice," Letta said. She felt rather than saw Danu and Rua tense.

Danu caught her hand. "You are Letta. The girl that killed John Noa." Danu's mouth hung open, astonishment written across her features.

"Are you?" Rua said. "Are you really?"

"I am," Letta said, so quietly she didn't know if they had heard her.

"May the Goddess bless you," Danu said, and Letta could hear the reverence in her voice.

"We often wondered what became of you," Rua said, "after the Water Tower. We had such hope."

"We all did," Letta said. "Maybe we were foolish."

"How can you say that," Danu said, "after all that happened? There must be hope. What do you plan to do next? We hear there are rebels gathering in the forest. Will you lead them?"

"I am not the person to lead us, Danu," Letta said, horrified. "I have no experience. I have already made mistakes. Terrible mistakes. We need someone older, wiser than me."

She saw the disappointment on their faces, but even as she heard herself speak, she knew the words were true. She didn't want to be a leader. She didn't even want to be the wordsmith anymore. She wanted to disappear.

"She's tired," she heard Marlo say. "It's been a long day. I think we should sleep."

"Of course," Danu said, but Letta could hear the defeat in her voice. "Letta can sleep in my tent, and you can sleep in Rua's."

Letta desperately wanted to say something to undo the damage, but the words stuck in her throat. She watched Danu and Rua banking down the fire, burying the remains of the pigeons, and thought how brave they were. She headed to the tent, regret almost choking her.

CHAPTER 11

In the morning Danu drew a detailed map that would lead them to Edgeware.

"Go safely," Rua said to Letta as he embraced her. "We will be praying for you."

Danu looked her straight in the eye and said, "You are our hero, Letta. Please don't give up."

And then they were gone. Letta reran Danu's words in her head. A hero? If they knew what she had done, if they knew how she had selfishly risked everyone's safety, they wouldn't think her a hero then.

Marlo touched her hand. "Let's get everything together and go find Edgeware," he said gently.

They walked on through the forest, carefully following Danu's map. They met no one and didn't even talk much. Letta felt tired and dispirited. Marlo had told her earlier that day that there were many like Rua and Danu, people living in the forest drinking poisoned water and resigned to their fate. They chose to live a short life in freedom rather than put up with the regime in Ark.

Letta realized that Rua and Danu would be dead before they saw another spring. Anger stirred in her. What right had Amelia to take their lives? The injustice of it scorched her heart.

As they drew nearer to Edgeware's cottage, the terrain became more familiar. Letta vividly remembered how she had followed Finn along this very path, hoping to find Benjamin. And they had found him. The last hours she had spent with him were forever etched in her memory, like an old familiar story that comforted her when nothing else could. The cottage appeared as it had on that night a year ago, but this time Edgeware was there, her back to them, foraging for food. Letta felt a rush of love and relief when she saw her and, throwing down her bag, ran to her.

The old woman turned. "Letta!"

And then they were holding each other in a tight embrace.

"Why you be here?" Edgeware said, examining both of them as if looking for clues.

"It's a long story," Letta said. "We need shelter, and we couldn't think where else to go."

"Come inside," Edgeware said. "Both of you. Come now."

She led them into the cottage with its low door and wooden floor, and there she brewed tea for them while she fixed a pot of soup. The smell of herbs and garlic filled the room.

"What are you really doing here, Letta?" she asked.

"I don't know," Letta said. "I don't want to stay in Ark. I suppose I could go and try to find my parents. Benjamin gave me their charts and their plans. But all of that is back in Ark."

"Why did you not go a year ago?"

Letta felt the blood rush to her face. "I was running schools, teaching the children language. We were planning... planning a revolution. The Creators wanted to overturn Amelia and—"

"We still do," Marlo interjected.

Edgeware looked at Letta. "But you do not?" she said softly.

"No," Letta said. "I am not the right person. I...I just mess things up. I make things worse, Edgeware."

Edgeware nodded. "This place will give you time to think, child. That is what you need. Time to make a plan. Now! Marlo, can you bring in some wood? Letta be helping me here."

Marlo nodded and went outside as Edgeware gathered up the soup bowls and spoons. Letta was desperate to change the subject, to talk about something other than herself.

"You've lived here a long time, haven't you, Edgeware?" she asked.

"Long enough," Edgeware answered. "I never be liking living with a lot of other people, so I be making my home here. Just me and my son, my Thomas. I be telling you his story when you be here before."

Letta tried to banish the image that came unbidden to her mind. Thomas had killed himself after Noa had removed his tongue in an effort to curb language. She could only imagine the horror Edgeware felt every time she thought about that.

Edgeware picked up a small wooden horse, perfectly formed. "He be making this for me when he be only ten. Thomas be loving the trees and he be loving music. That be his flute over there."

Letta looked and saw a beautiful wooden flute on a shelf on the far side of the room.

"I killed a gavver, Edgeware." The words seemed to find their own way out of her mouth. "I didn't do it purposely. I thought it would injure him, not kill him."

Edgeware nodded. "And now they be looking for you?"

Letta nodded.

"You poor child. This is nay the life you would have asked for."

"I wish Benjamin were still here," Letta managed to say. "I don't want to be the one people depend on. I don't want to be a hero. I don't even know if I want to be the wordsmith."

"I see that," Edgeware said. "And yet you already be a hero. You be showing courage and leadership. Those things made you a hero to many people."

"I made mistakes, Edgeware. Mistakes that almost cost Marlo his life and cost his friends their freedom."

"And yet Marlo still be alive."

"No thanks to me."

Edgeware got up slowly and lit a candle.

"I wonder what Benjamin be saying to you if he be here now?" she said.

"I don't know," Letta said. "He seems so far away."

A white butterfly flew in through the open window and hovered for a second over the wooden horse's head. Edgeware watched it, puckered her lips, and blew on it. "Some say white butterflies be the souls of the dead," she said.

"Really?" Letta said, watching the gossamer wings flit in and out of the light.

Edgeware yawned, stretching her body in the chair. The door opened and Marlo came in.

"I lit the torches while I was out there," he said.

Letta remembered how Edgeware lit a circle of fire around the cottage each night to keep wild animals away.

"Thank you," Edgeware said. "I be going to bed. Letta, you can sleep upstairs. Marlo can go up to the loft. Good night, you both."

Letta watched Edgeware as she shuffled across the floor

to the little annex off the main room. The butterfly fluttered around her head, and she swatted it gently with her hand.

As soon as she was gone, Letta turned to Marlo. "White butterflies are the souls of the dead. Do you believe that?" she whispered.

"If it's true, this planet would be covered in them," Marlo said.

"She loved her son very much," Letta said, her eyes lingering on the wooden horse. "She must miss him terribly."

The silence stretched between them, each one remembering their own loved ones. When Letta looked up, she found Marlo's eyes looking back at her, and once more she was struck by their beauty. He held out his hand to her, and she put her own hand in his. He caressed it with his thumb. Letta felt her very bones would melt.

"She's a great talker, Edgeware," he said with a smile.

"Yes," said Letta. "I like that."

"Me too," Marlo said, looking away from her. "I've always liked the way you speak as well."

Letta felt her heart jump. "Have you?" she managed to say.

He looked at her now, his eyes glowing softly in the candlelight. "Yes," he said. "I have."

Now it was Letta's turn to look away. She could feel the heat of his stare even though she couldn't see him. "Thank you," she said, and her throat hurt for all the words she wanted to say but couldn't.

"We're going to survive this, Letta," Marlo said softly. "I know we are." He smiled at her and her heart raced. He touched her cheek lightly. "Get some sleep," he said.

Letta stood up slowly. She wanted to stay there all night, talking to him, holding him. "Good night," she said.

"Good night," said Marlo, and she felt his eyes follow her as she picked her way across the room to the little stairs and started to climb the narrow steps.

The room was small and dark and empty except for a chair and a makeshift bed of hay covered with a thin blanket in the corner. Letta sat on it and replayed the scene downstairs again and again. Her mind was in turmoil. She didn't know what to think about Marlo. He was her friend, but was he more than that? What did he think of her?

She took off her outer layer of clothing and placed everything neatly on the chair. Then she kicked off her shoes, happy to be able to free her feet. She lay down on the bed. There was a faint smell of lavender in the room, and she found it comforting. Lavender, her mother's smell. Her eyes closed, and sleep swept her blissfully away.

Four hours later, the night was firmly established with a big moon hanging in a black sky. Letta was dreaming of home when a noise woke her. She sat up quickly. Someone had opened her bedroom door. She stayed absolutely still, her heart thudding, waiting.

"Letta!" A tiny whisper. Marlo.

In a second, he was beside her.

"We have to get out," he said in a voice so small Letta had to strain to hear him. She froze. She could feel his fear. "Gavvers. Downstairs."

Letta could hear them. Men with loud, deep voices beneath her somewhere. She couldn't take it in. They had found her and Marlo already. And she had led them to Edgeware. She jumped out of her bed and rearranged it so it looked as it had when she'd entered the room earlier. She felt cold all over. She pulled on her shoes and the clothes she had thrown on the chair. She took her satchel and looked at Marlo expectantly. He was surveying the room. There was nowhere to hide.

Letta ran to the window and looked out. In a heartbeat, Marlo was beside her. He grabbed the old window and jerked it up. It moved a tiny fraction, then stopped. Marlo yanked it again. The window creaked but opened. A blast of cold air filled the room. Marlo pulled a knife from his belt and cut away some of the clinging ivy.

Downstairs, the voices were getting louder. She looked at the window again, her palms sweating, her head light. She had no choice, she told herself.

She closed her eyes, tried to breathe. She felt Marlo take her hand. She climbed onto the windowsill, clutching the frame with cold fingers. She looked through the window and down into the dark void below. She could imagine losing her grip and plummeting into the blackness beneath. Somewhere in the distance a dog howled at the moon, and Letta felt the world tip dizzily.

Marlo held her tight. She put one foot out. Her stomach lurched. She glanced down. By the light of the moon, she could see the ground far below. She grabbed hold of the main stem of the ivy and carefully lifted her other foot out. A crash from inside the house almost made her jump clean off the wall.

"Move!" Marlo hissed. "They're coming!"

Letta put one foot down on the vine and found a foothold. Marlo swung himself out the window, his shoe almost crushing her hand. He closed the window behind him, costing them more precious seconds. From inside, Letta could hear people stamping up the stairs. She thought she heard Edgeware scream.

She took another step down, found a foothold, then a handhold. Sweat had started to run down her forehead and seep into her eyes so that she could no longer see clearly. She took another step. Her foot slipped on the wet vine and then she was sliding, arms and legs torn by the thorny climber underneath the ivy. She wanted to scream but knew she couldn't.

Down and down she went, legs tearing, hands burning. It took all her concentration not to let go. Finally, the vine ended, and she plummeted to the ground. Pain shot through her hip. She stifled the cry, allowing only one sob to escape her lips. She had landed in a grassy ditch under the front window. She looked up. Marlo had stopped climbing halfway down and was hanging there, his body pressed against the wall, stock-still in the moonlight.

Above his head, Letta saw the shape of a man leaning out the window as far as he could. She crouched lower, pushing her body down into the ditch, hoping the long grass would hide her from their sight.

"Nothing!" the man's voice said, spitting the word into the night. Letta didn't dare breathe. There was no sign of Edgeware. Had they killed her? It was illegal to harbor criminals. They could shoot her, and no one would blame them. What had she done? If they killed Edgeware, the blood would be on her hands. More blood. She was the one who had brought them to the old woman's door.

The pain in her hip was throbbing now, but she didn't care. She couldn't tear her eyes away from Marlo.

A few seconds later, the door of the cottage crashed open and two gavvers came out.

"Come on!" the tall one in front called over his shoulder. He was within feet of her. *If he turns around, he'll see me*, Letta thought. *If they search the garden, they will find us. If they look up…* She closed her eyes. They had stopped at the gate and were talking. Their voices were too low for Letta to catch what they said. Why didn't they just go? She felt an urge to scream to relieve the tension. Then she heard them moving away down the road. Still she didn't move.

Somewhere overhead, an owl screamed, making her jump in fright.

Then, nothing. No sign of Edgeware.

Fear, cold as the moon, bubbled up from somewhere deep inside her. Letta watched numbly as Marlo shinnied down the side of the house. Within seconds, he was beside her.

"Are you hurt?" he asked, taking her hand between both of his.

"I'm fine," she managed to say. "Edgeware! Go and see…"

Marlo nodded. Letta watched him go, her heart pounding. She had to get up. Slowly and painfully, she pulled herself into a standing position. Her hands were bleeding, and she could feel the warm trickle of blood on her thighs. A figure appeared in the door ahead of her. Edgeware! For a second, she forgot her pain and rushed to the older woman. "You're all right!" she said.

Edgeware's face was grim.

"Which be more than I can say for you," she said, taking Letta's arm and helping her into the house. "Boil water!" she said to Marlo. "I be needing to clean those cuts. We have nay much time. They'll come back. They know there be no man here. They'll come and steal—or worse. I will pack some food."

The next half hour was a blur to Letta. Edgeware bathed her cut hands and legs with herbs and warm water and applied bandages of soft, sweet-smelling moss. Then, taking as much food and water as they could carry, they all left the house.

"That's it! We walk," Edgeware said, striding out ahead of them. Marlo and Letta had no choice but to follow.

"Which way they be gone?" Edgeware asked.

"That way," Letta said, pointing in the direction she had seen them go.

"North—good," was all Edgeware said, and she started off in the opposite direction.

Letta tried to find out more about where they were going, but Edgeware would not be drawn. "Less you know, less you can tell" was all she said, and Letta knew from the tone of her voice that there was no use arguing.

The night was still dark, and Letta had to give all her attention to keeping up with the other two. Every part of her hurt, and walking was as much hardship as she could bear.

"What did they want?" she finally managed to ask Edgeware.

"They be looking for a girl and a boy. A girl who be after killing a gavver."

"Did they hurt you?" Letta asked, holding her breath.

"No," Edgeware said. "Not my body."

Letta tried to imagine what that meant. She didn't want to ask. She remembered the little wooden horse and the beautiful flute and knew there were worse things than cuts and bruises. They walked through the night till the dawn broke. Edgeware took them down byroads within the forest, lonely overgrown places, but even so, they were constantly watching for the gavvers. After what seemed like a very long time, the day dawned, moodily at first, and then the sun came out, warming Letta's bones.

Ahead of them, Letta could see a small village, poor, pinched houses huddled together. They were all houses from before the Melting, made from blocks and timber. Nowadays, houses were made from earth and wattles, insulated with sheep's wool. As they got closer, Letta could see the houses had once had little gardens, and flowers still bloomed there as if in memory of that time. There must be bees here, Letta thought. Bees had become almost extinct years before the Melting, killed by insecticides and other poisons. Without bees there had been no pollination, no flowers. John Noa's scientists had managed to reintroduce bees just before the Earth was struck by the last disasters. The species was struggling now, but some of the little creatures were managing to survive in Ark.

Letta looked again at the garden. The flowers were in bloom, violet, pink, and winter white. She didn't know their names, but she couldn't help admiring them. She had once learned the names of twelve garden flowers. Benjamin had found a box full of empty seed packets in the attic of an old house. He had salvaged all of the names.

Tulip, primrose, delphinium.

She had no idea that there were such places in the forest. She had been brought up to believe the forest was a terrifying place. No one had said there were places like this among the trees.

She hurried to catch up with Edgeware. "Does nobody live in those houses?" she asked.

"No one," Edgeware said. "Long be gone."

They came to a small bridge. Half of it lay in the river, but with some effort, Letta managed to clamber over. Ahead of them was a tall stone building with a steeple.

"A church," Edgeware said without waiting for the question. "Before the Melting, people believed in gods. This be a shrine to one of them."

God: *idol, deity, supreme being.*

Letta thought of all the people who secretly worshipped the statue of the Goddess in Ark. "Can we look inside?" she asked.

"Nay much to see," Edgeware said.

"Please?" Letta begged. She didn't know why, but she wanted to go in. She wanted it badly.

Marlo frowned. "I don't think we should delay," he said to Edgeware.

"He be right," Edgeware said with a frown. "We should keep moving."

"Please," Letta said. "I have never been in one, but Benjamin told me about them."

Edgeware paused for a moment, then shrugged. "One minute," she said. "Marlo, go with her."

Letta didn't wait to hear any more. She ran toward the door of the building and went through. There were only two walls left standing, empty spaces where windows had once been, an earth floor and a roof full of holes. The floor was strewn with rubble, the air full of dust. Letta walked carefully to the far side of the great room. The remaining walls were decorated with faded, chalky pictures in soft pinks and softer blues. Pictures of winged creatures with halos of light around their heads that seemed to be falling from the sky. There was an altar, a big piece of marble, and above it the remains of a window.

Not just any window. Letta gasped and looked at Marlo. He was equally entranced. The window was made of colored glass. A picture of a dove remained and, below it, three falling leaves. The sun shone through them and made them seem almost magical. The colors bounced onto the altar, blue and red and orange. Letta had never seen anything like it.

"It's...it's beautiful," she managed to say. Other words ricocheted around the window.

Glorious, lustrous, brilliant.

The building had an air of peace about it. Letta

thought she could feel the ghosts of people's prayers lingering in the stone walls. She tried to imagine what it was like to believe in a god. To have someone to pray to, something to believe in. It reminded her of the Goddess in Ark. There were people who believed in her, too, but Letta had never been one of them.

"We'd better go." Marlo's voice was soft beside her.

Letta nodded, though in her heart she didn't want to leave.

"Carmina would love this place," Marlo said, and Letta saw his eyes cloud over. "I dreamed about her last night. I dreamed she was singing in a gilded cage."

"Didn't you once tell me there was truth in dreams?" Letta said.

"If you know where to look."

He looked so sad. Letta struggled to find words that might comfort him. "Finn will take care of her," she said at last.

What was Finn doing now? Was he languishing in a prison cell, or had they banished him? Killed him?

"I know he will. He's been my father since I was seven years old," Marlo said. "My father and he were best friends. When my dad was lost…" He hesitated, then looked at Letta and smiled. "He understands me, I suppose," he said. "Or he tries to. I dreamed about him too. I hope he is safe."

The air between them crackled with emotion.

"We should go," Marlo said softly. He turned and walked

down the old aisle of the church. In a trance, she followed him out into the sunshine.

At midday, Edgeware stopped at a crossroads and looked around, a small frown playing across her forehead. "I nay recall this," she said. "I think we go this way." She turned left down a rough track. In just a few minutes, trees and grasses swallowed them up. Edgeware stopped and sniffed the air. "Do you be smelling it?" she said to Letta.

"Smell what?"

The old woman sniffed again. "The earth," she said. "I smell moss and earth and twigs. It be going to rain."

"Really?" Letta said. "You're sure?"

The old woman pointed toward the western sky and Letta saw a rainbow, its colors bright, infused with light.

"A storm," Edgeware said simply. "A rainbow in the west means a storm. Always did. Always will."

Edgeware hurried on and Letta followed her, stumbling on the rough ground, almost falling a number of times. Her back was wet with the weight of the bags on her back, and her hip still ached from her fall the previous night.

Suddenly, they came to another clearing and in front of them was a house. A square gray box with a tin roof. The door was nothing but a series of planks roughly nailed together. Letta stopped.

Edgeware shook her head. "We should have gone the other way at the crossroads. I nay be seeing this before."

Letta walked up to the house and squinted through a cloudy window. There was no one inside. "Should we go in for a look?"

Edgeware had already started to take off her heavy bags. "We be needing to eat something," she said. "Go see what you can find, Marlo."

Marlo put down his own bags and went to do Edgeware's bidding.

Letta couldn't resist. She tried the door. It creaked open. Cautiously, she went inside. It was a big, open room, quite dark, with deep shadows in every corner. The walls were covered in something yellow and faded. She went closer.

"Edgeware!" Letta's scream shattered the silence. Edgeware came running with Marlo right behind her. They stopped dead when they saw Letta.

"What?" Marlo said. "What?"

Shakily, Letta pointed to the wall. Edgeware and Marlo moved in closer.

"What is it?" Marlo asked, rubbing his hands gently along the wall.

"They're *words*," Letta said. "Words."

"I still don't understand," Marlo said. "What is it?"

"It's newspaper," Letta said. "They had it before the Melting so that wordsmiths could tell people what was happening in the world."

She rubbed her hand along the paper pasted to the wall, still not believing her good fortune. This was a treasure trove. She grabbed her satchel and took out her paper, her ink, and her pen.

Edgeware's voice pulled her up short. "Letta!" she said. "We must be leaving here now. There be no knowing what kind of people be living here."

Letta felt panic rise in her chest. "But…I need to record this. There are bound to be words here we no longer have."

Edgeware shook her head. "I be sorry, girl," she said. "We need to go now."

"Maybe I can help her," Marlo said. "Just ten minutes, please."

Silence. Finally, Edgeware spoke. "My writing nay be too good, girl, but I'll help too if I can. We must be quick."

Edgeware and Marlo took up positions in front of the wall. Letta gave them pens, and they began to transcribe what they saw. Letta found an advertisement for something and copied down the words. Something caught her eye farther up the wall.

John Noa.

Her heart quickened. It was an article about John Noa written before the Melting. She leaned her hand against the wall and started to read.

The lunatic ambitions of climate-change fanatic and member of the government John Noa are reaching new heights. These ambitions pose a serious danger to human survival, the very objective they claim to champion. Among the latest unhinged proposals are "cloud ships" to generate more cloud and deflect the sun's rays. This plan envisions thousands of wind-powered ships cruising through the oceans, creating bad weather. This extraordinary idea is not as radical as his other famous plan to launch mirrors into space to deflect the sun. We should count ourselves lucky that this deranged idea to switch off the light that sustains life on Earth is too expensive to be implemented. Man-made global warming is a fantasy. Climate change is ongoing and is nothing new. The same cannot be said for the irresponsible plans of Mr. Noa, whose ego has completely outstripped his limited knowledge. For now, the real danger is not that man-made climate change will actually take place but that this

global-warming alarmist himself will engineer it.
In short, global warming will not kill us, but
fanatics like Noa and his followers could well do so.

Some of the words in the article were new to Letta, words like *radical* and *fanatic*, but she got the general message. Noa had not been a popular man before the Melting. Reading the article again, Letta was amazed at the arrogance of the reporter who claimed that global warming was a fantasy. Some fantasy! Noa had been right about global warming, even if he had been wrong about so much else. She was anxious to share this new information with Marlo, but she was even more anxious to make sure they recorded all the words from the wall. Talking to Marlo would have to wait. The new information occupied most of her thought processes as she continued her work.

"What's this?" Marlo's voice had an edge of excitement. He was pointing at pages that were lining the stairs.

Letta walked over and stood in shock looking at them. Lists and lists of words and their definitions. She knew what it was. It had been called a dictionary. A sort of word book. She ran her hand along the page. This section had words beginning with the letter *G*.

Gab (verb): talk at length.
"Celeste was gabbing about the
country before the war."

Synonyms: chatter, chitter-chatter, chat, talk, gossip, gabble, babble, prattle, jabber, blather, blab.

Apart from "talk" they didn't have any of those words. Letta was sure of it. Her heart pounded in her chest. She had to record them, quickly.

She felt Edgeware come up behind her.

"Time we be goin'," she said. "I nay like the sound of that wind."

Letta shook her head. They couldn't leave now. She heard Edgeware go to the door and open it, even as her pencil flew across the page.

"Letta!" Edgeware called to her.

Letta turned. A wintry gust drove a cloud of leaves into the house. Edgeware bent and picked one up. Letta watched her as she examined it closely, turning it over between her fingers, holding it to her nose, and inhaling its smell. Just then, Letta heard a loud rumble. Thunder. A forked flash of lightning hit the ground outside, sending sparks flying in all directions.

Edgeware closed the door quickly. "Storm or no storm, we better be gettin' away from here. There's no knowin' who be living here or what they might be doing if they come back and be finding strangers in their house. Come on!"

Letta reluctantly turned to the door. How could she leave now? The house was a treasure trove of words. If she didn't record them, they could be lost forever.

"Letta!" Marlo's voice woke her from her reverie. "We can come back another time. You know where this place is now. Don't look so heartbroken."

"All right," she said, but her mind was in turmoil. How could she get back here? She had to record the words. That was her duty. She might not be able to do anything else, but she could do this. For Benjamin. For herself.

The wind was rising. Edgeware stood still, listening. Without warning, she spun around, nearly knocking Letta off balance. "Hide!" she said. "Someone coming."

Letta looked around in desperation. Hide where?

"Over there," Marlo whispered. "Move back into the trees."

Edgeware grabbed Letta's hand, and they followed Marlo into the gloom of the forest. They kept well back, hidden in the shadows, waiting to run should the need arise. Edgeware nudged Letta. "There he be," she said. "A man."

Letta looked out through a gap in the trees. She could just make him out. He was a heavy-set, round-shouldered man with long, shaggy, unkempt hair. He was dressed in a long coat and had a hat pulled down over his ears. In his hand, he held a live rabbit. The rabbit was bucking and twisting, trying to get free, but the man held it by the legs, giving it no chance to escape. As Letta watched, he pulled back his arm and hit the rabbit on the corner of the house. Letta gasped and made a move as if to stop him, but Edgeware held her fast.

"Stay!" she hissed at the distressed girl. "Stay!"

Letta forced herself to calm down. The man drew back his arm and hit the screaming animal again and again until the creature stopped moving. He threw the body into a bucket by the door before going inside.

"Move!" Edgeware said, pushing Letta before her. "We need be getting out of here before he be seeing us."

Letta didn't wait to be told again. Together, they crept out of their hiding place and made for the road.

"We need be getting back to that cross," Edgeware said. "We can be walking all afternoon and be setting camp in the evening. I be knowin' a place. Then, in the morning, it be a half day's journey to where we need to go."

Letta could barely hear her above the wind. "Where, Edgeware? Where are we going?"

"A rebel camp. This crowd move around, but they been in this one spot a few months."

"Really?" Letta said, excitement mounting in her chest.

"I nay know how long they be staying there. We can't delay."

The rest of that day was spent walking, battling wind and rain. Shadows flitted through the trees. Letta thought she saw badgers, rats, deer. The trees whipped branches into their faces, and brambles and nettles dogged every step. She heard birds shout warning cries and wished they would shout a warning to them, too, should they need it. By late afternoon, the wind had dropped and the rain had become a damp mist, but the air was sweet and cool.

The walking seemed easier now. At one point, Letta looked over to her left and saw a graveyard of vehicles from before the Melting—cars, buses, trucks. They lay in neat rows, falling apart with rust. Letta couldn't help thinking they had also played a part in destroying the planet. It was hard to believe people had once owned them, driven them, fed them with gas, knowing the oil they were burning was adding to the global-warming crisis. She shrugged. The planet suddenly felt lonely. So many had died. So many were gone.

Her mind went back to the words papering the walls of the house. A dictionary. Or part of one. A relic from the past. Something irreplaceable.

A few minutes later, they came to a clearing.

"Will we make camp here?" Marlo asked the older woman.

"Might as well," Edgeware said, throwing the bags on the ground. "Safe as any."

Letta put her hand to her shoulder and took off her own bag, then threw it on the ground. But her mind was somewhere else. She had made her decision. She was going back. Back to the house, back to record the words. And no one was going to stop her.

CHAPTER 12

#148

NIGHT

TIME AFTER SUNSET

Letta turned and looked back the way she had come. Half a day's walk away.

Edgeware started to collect twigs to make a fire. Marlo and Letta organized the rations they had and made up beds for the night.

Later, after Edgeware had made a small fire and they'd shared a pot of soup, Letta sat watching the sun go down and the shadows lengthen all around them. There was little conversation. As soon as she could, Letta withdrew from the other two and pretended to settle down to sleep. Her thoughts were racing, darting like minnows around her head. How could she live with herself if she cost the world its last hold on language? She had to go back and finish what she had started. There had to be a way.

Relief surged through her now that the decision was made. There was no point in involving Marlo or Edgeware. They would never agree to it. She would wait till they were asleep and then she would go. When she had recorded the words, she'd follow them to the camp.

She lay there, listening to the sounds of birds and animals all around winding down for the night. Marlo and Edgeware talked quietly. Letta heard snatches of their conversation, but she couldn't concentrate. Finally, after about an hour, she heard them wishing each other good night.

She waited until she could hear Edgeware snoring, her breath rising and falling like the waves of the sea. Then she knew it was time.

She stood up. She waited for a second to see if the others had been disturbed. Nothing. Good, she thought and turned to face west and head back over the road they had just traveled. Edgeware had set a circle of torches around their camp, and as she left, Letta took one of them with her. It might be useful if she met a wild animal.

A full moon lit her way. Edgeware had told her that the full moon in the second month had been called the *snow moon* in the time before the Melting. Letta liked that and was glad of the moon's bright company as she walked. All around were strange noises, strange smells, and the constant threat of attack. The shadows that had flitted through the trees in the afternoon were now made solid.

A fox blocked her path at one stage, a large male. His red coat was lit by the moon, and his eyes glinted with curiosity. Letta brandished the torch and he turned lazily, slipping away with tiny, elegant steps. Later, she came on a whole herd of deer standing in the moonlight. They looked as though they were waiting for something, standing shoulder to shoulder, in silence. But there was menace there too. She heard low growls and shrill screams as she pushed herself on. Things scuttled by her feet, and heavier bodies tramped through the brush just out of sight.

Her thoughts flew to Marlo and Edgeware. She realized how much she had come to depend on them. Especially Marlo. But not anymore. This was something she had to do for herself. For most of the journey she was in a state of high anxiety, but all fear was overruled by the desperate need she had to record the words.

As morning dawned, she knew she was within two or three hours of the newspaper house. She threw away the torch. She was exhausted, thirsty and weak with hunger, but she didn't care. She just wanted to get there and retrieve the words.

Letta reached the house well before midday. Her heart leapt at the sight of it, standing there just as they had left it. Letta hid in the bushes due north of it and watched. Nothing. The house seemed to be deserted. But how could she go in? What if the man was inside? Should she wait till nightfall? She didn't think she could. She would go into the house. If he was there, she'd pretend to be a traveler looking for a drink. Cautiously, she headed for the door.

She had to break cover at the northern gable of the house and run across the old cobbled yard to the front door. Out in the open, she felt vulnerable. *This is how a wild creature must feel*, she thought, *when it breaks away from its natural habitat. Exposed.* The bucket was still there. Letta glanced at it. It was empty except for a dark smear of blood near the handle. She took a deep breath and knocked at the door. Silence. Nothing moved inside.

She could smell the faint sickly smell of garlic. She waited. He must be out. Hunting, probably. She turned the handle, and the door opened noisily. Letta looked inside. The papered walls looked back at her. She took a step over the threshold. Her heart soared. She would work quickly and be long gone before he got back. She pulled open the door and ducked inside.

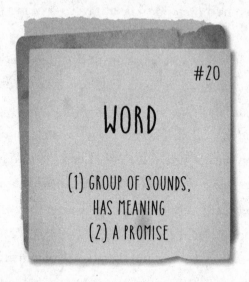

CHAPTER 13

#20

WORD

(1) GROUP OF SOUNDS,
HAS MEANING
(2) A PROMISE

She opened her satchel and took out her paper, her pen, and her small bottle of ink. The pervading smell in the house was of mold and damp, and Letta knew that the paper wouldn't last forever. In places it was torn and peeling, and it would take time to decipher what was written there. She had to grab as many words as she possibly could. And soon she was lost in her own world—looking, writing, looking again.

Then a hand was slapped across her mouth and her neck yanked so violently, she almost passed out with the pain. She tried to scream, but she couldn't make a sound. Behind her, she heard a man grunt, a low, guttural sound, then he dragged her toward the door on the far side of the room. With a heavy-booted foot, he kicked the door open.

Letta struggled against him, trying to pull her head away

from his heavy hand, but he was far stronger. Images of the man killing the rabbit flashed through her mind, and she desperately tried to suppress them. She stopped struggling. She could hear him breathing. Slow, regular breaths. The smell of old sweat filled her nose, sharp and acrid. She was in a small bedroom. In the beam of light from the open door, she saw a mound of hay on the floor, covered in dirty-looking blankets. There was one small window boarded up. Besides that, the room was empty except for a chair. He threw her onto it. Now she could see him properly.

His dirty brown hair fell over one eye. His eyes, when she managed to look into them, were green and full of a mad kind of intelligence, bright, piercing. One of his eyebrows was constantly raised as if in a perpetual question. A smile played on his lips, *No*, Letta thought, *not a smile, a sneer.* He was so close to her now that she could feel his breath on her face. He grabbed the two arms of the chair and brought his face very close to hers.

"Who you?" he said in a rusty voice, a spray of spittle hitting her cheek as he spoke. She knew at once that he had very little language.

"I am Letta," she said slowly. "I mean no harm. I would… would like a drink." She made a conscious effort to speak very slowly and clearly. She knew from experience that people who were poor speakers still understood language very well. "Please."

He stared at her, saying nothing. Then, he straightened up and waved his hand at her. "Stay!" he said.

It was then she noticed the hook on the wall and the rope hanging from it. The man removed the rope and came back to her. His hands were callused, she noticed, a worker's hands. He threw the rope around her, almost gently, and within seconds she was securely tied to the chair. He stepped back to look at her. He made a high clicking noise with his tongue. Letta heard the scratching of nails on the wooden floor. A dog? Her eyes were riveted to the door. And suddenly he was there. A wolf. Thick gray fur. A long muzzle. His lips were pulled back revealing short yellow teeth. He was huge, and she could smell the thick, damp fug of wet fur. The man clicked again, and the wolf walked over to him and sat at his feet. The man smiled.

"Stay!" he said, and the wolf turned his yellow eyes to her and growled low in his throat. The animal's tongue was hanging from his mouth. His keen eyes stared at her as if he could read her mind. Letta felt a cold shiver crawl across her skin. The yellow teeth were visible behind the heavy lips. She tried not to move a muscle.

The man stood back and examined the scene. It seemed to please him. He laughed. A rough, dry sound. "Good," he said. "Very good."

Then he turned around and left, closing the door behind him. The room was plunged into darkness. Letta could no longer see the animal, but she could feel him and hear him breathing.

For the first hour she didn't move. Her muscles burned with tension. The rope had started to bite into her upper arms, but all of her discomfort paled beside her terror of the wolf. Once her eyes had adjusted to the dark, she could see his gray fur and bright eyes. *I have to do something*, her brain was telling her. *He's only an animal.* He had barely moved since the man left. She decided to speak to him.

"G-good boy," she said, her voice hoarse.

He pricked his ears and gave a small growl, showing his teeth. She pulled back in the chair, trying to put more distance between them. Her head filled with images of the wolf tearing her limb from limb. *I have to do this*, she said to herself. *It's my only chance.* She needed to speak to him in a steady voice. She couldn't let him see she was afraid.

"Good boy," she said again, her voice stronger now. "Good boy. Stay."

The wolf stared back at her, unflinching, but he didn't growl.

"Good boy," Letta said again. "Sit!"

He didn't move. He stood there staring at her, but somehow he seemed less interested. She had to think of a way out. The man would have to untie her at some stage, and maybe then she could make a run for it. Her mind raced, trying to work out a plan, but she couldn't know how the man would react or what he wanted from her. She struggled against the ropes. The wolf cocked his ears at her sudden movement. Just as Letta was about to speak to the animal again, she heard voices outside.

The front door opened, and now she could clearly hear

two men talking. One voice she recognized as her captor's. "I come tomorrow," he said.

"You know what we need?" the other man said, and Letta knew immediately that he was a person with language.

"Yes," the first man answered. "For babies..."

"Yes. Herbs for the babies. The usual. Go to the gate. Wait there. Do not go inside."

"Yes. Understand. No go inside."

"Tonight, then?"

"Tonight."

The door outside opened and closed. The visitor was gone. Letta struggled against the rope, trying to loosen it before her captor came back in. The wolf growled. A warning. She ignored him. His hackles rose. Letta yanked her right arm with all the strength she could muster. The knot loosened a little. The wolf growled again, deep in his throat. Letta made another effort to free her arm, sweat trickling into her eyes. The wolf took a step back. Letta locked eyes with him, and then he sprang.

CHAPTER 14

#72

LOST

MISSING, NO LONGER HAVE

She felt his claws first, sharp nails digging into the skin of her shoulders. The force of his weight knocked the chair over, and Letta found herself looking at the ceiling. The heat from the wolf was overpowering. She could smell his fetid breath, feel his heart racing. She tried to scream but could find no voice. Her head was full of words, but she couldn't make a sound.

Vicious, bloodthirsty.

She kicked out with her legs, the only part of her body she had any control over. The wolf didn't even seem to notice. She felt the nails again on her ribs. The animal snarled and snapped at her face, spittle flying into her eyes.

Letta screamed. Her screaming seemed to drive the wolf

into a frenzy. Growling and snarling, he threw himself on her again. She heard her dress tear, felt warm blood run down her arm. The snarling was at fever pitch. He was making so much noise that Letta didn't hear the man at first.

"Stop!" he roared. "Stop, boy!"

The wolf turned his head to look at where the order had come from. The next thing she knew, the animal was being pulled away from her.

"Lie down!" the man roared at the wolf. "Down!"

Letta thought she heard the wolf whimper. Then the man was hauling her and the chair back up to their original position. Letta felt her stomach heave. She retched but there was no food to throw up. When she looked up again, the man was watching her, and the wolf was slinking out the door into the kitchen. She dropped her chin to her chest, exhausted.

The man approached her. She jumped. What was he going to do now? He started to undo the rope. "Sleep!" he said, pointing at the pile of hay. "Sleep!"

She noticed he used the same tone with her as he did with the wolf. She could barely stand up. Her knees wobbled when she put her weight on the floor. She was sure she would fall, but she managed to walk to the bed. She sat on the mattress and looked up at him. "What are you going to do with me?" she said. "Why are you keeping me?"

No answer. He turned and left the room. Minutes later he came back with a tin can of water, a cup, and a slice of dark bread. Letta heard him turn a key in the bedroom door after he left.

She drank thirstily from the cup. The water was clear and cold. The bread tasted of rye and age. Letta chewed it carefully. She examined her wounds, mostly deep scratches on her arms and chest and ribs. She cleaned them as best she could with what remained in the tin can. She lay on the makeshift bed, her thoughts in turmoil. Her ribs hurt from the wolf's claws. Her head throbbed.

She had no idea what she was going to do. In the morning, the man might hand her over to the gavvers. Had the gavvers been here already looking for her? Panic rose in her chest, squeezing her lungs. She had to escape. She had to. But how? She had no doubt the wolf and his master were on the other side of the door. The thought of the earlier attack sent her into a cold sweat. She shivered. She stood up and examined the window. It was boarded up from the outside. She tried to push against the boards, but it was pointless. Had she survived so much for it to finish like this? She lay down and tried to sleep, but she couldn't relax. It had grown even darker in the room, and all noises had ceased outside. Suddenly, she remembered the snippet of conversation she had heard between the man and his visitor. The stranger had been talking about babies—*herbs for the babies*. What could that mean? What babies were out here in the middle of the forest? Had it something to do with the babies from Ark? She turned on her side, trying to get comfortable. As she turned, she heard a faint scratching. At first, she thought she had imagined it. Then she heard it again, louder now. Was it the wolf? She stood up. Her eyes peered into the darkness. Nothing.

There it was again. It seemed to be coming from the direction of the window. She walked toward the boarded-up opening. Something scraping against the boards. A bear? Should she call out? Would the man come and help her? Was he even in the house? Her eyes had begun to adjust to the dark. She was certain one of the boards on the window had moved. There! It moved again. What was she to do? As she watched, the board suddenly gave way altogether. She gasped.

"Letta?"

It took her a second to process what was happening.

"Marlo?"

She felt like she was in a dream. How could it be Marlo?

"Letta!" he said again. "I'll pull out another board. You should be able to get through then, I think…"

Moonlight snaked in through the new opening in the window. Letta leaned on the sill and pulled herself up. Within seconds, she was standing on the grass.

Marlo caught her roughly by the arm. "Come on," he said, "Let's go!"

"I can't," Letta said. "My bag. It's still in there."

"Your bag? Are you serious?"

"The words are in it, Marlo. The words I came back to

get. It's not just the bag—there's something else. I'll explain later."

Marlo frowned. "We have to get out of here. You're lucky he didn't kill you already. Where is the bag?"

"Front room," Letta said. "There's a wolf in there."

Marlo raised an eyebrow. She thought she saw the shadow of a smile. "Of course," he said. "A wolf."

"Come on," Letta said. "We'll go around to the front."

She jumped up and, bent over, scuttled around to the front of the house.

Reluctantly, Marlo followed. Seconds later, they were crouched together in the scrub in front of the cottage, looking at the door.

"You said you had another reason?" Marlo whispered.

"He's up to something. Something to do with the missing babies in Ark. I just want to see what he does."

They crouched in the dense shrubbery in the front garden and watched.

The front door opened. The man took bundles of herbs from the step outside and pushed them into a cloth sack, the wolf at his side.

Herbs for the babies.

The wolf raised his head and sniffed the air. He growled. The man looked around. The wolf growled again. Letta noticed that the man had him on some kind of leash. The wolf was looking in their direction now. He growled again and put his snout in the air and howled. He was pulling on the leash, trying to get at them.

The man peered into the moonlit countryside. "What? What, boy?" He bent to release the animal from the lead.

Letta grabbed Marlo's hand. "We have to run," she said. "He knows we're here."

As she said the words, a rabbit broke cover and ran straight across the path of the wolf. The wolf went for it, dragging the man with him. The man yanked on the rope, pulling the wolf so vigorously the animal's two front paws left the ground.

"Come on!" the man roared at him and, pulling the wolf after him, set off toward the north, back toward the camp. But where Letta had followed the road, the man was going cross-country. Letta stayed where she was, afraid to move.

Marlo touched her hand. "I'll get your satchel," he said. "And then let's go."

He was back in seconds, the bag in his hand.

"Ready?" he said.

Letta wanted to go with him, but something held her back.

"What is it?" Marlo asked, seeing her hesitate.

"I think I should follow him," she said, slipping her bag onto her shoulder.

"Follow him? Are you mad? We have to get back. Edgeware doesn't know how long the rebels will be at the camp we're supposed to be heading for. She's gone on ahead to try to delay them."

Letta felt as though her heart was being ripped from her body. She wanted nothing more than to go with Marlo, and yet...

"There's something strange going on here," she said. "Remember Marta telling Finn about missing babies? And Thaddeus's story about the neighbor's missing baby? Mrs. Pepper from Central Kitchen told me that gavvers took the tanner's grandson. Then Rua and Danu mentioned stolen infants. And now this madman is talking about babies in the middle of the forest. I want to see for myself what's going on. I really need to know, Marlo."

Marlo frowned. "Do you know where he is going?"

Letta shook her head. "He's delivering herbs to babies. It might not be far."

"I'll go with you, but if he goes farther than an hour away, we should turn back."

"All right," Letta said and smiled at him.

He smiled back. "Let's go."

They could just make out the shape of the man crossing the fields with the wolf at his heels.

"We'd better not get too near them," Letta said. "The wolf will pick up our scent."

They walked on, not speaking in case their voices carried on the night air. Letta was so happy to be with Marlo that she didn't want to talk anyway. They came to a low stone wall. Marlo climbed over it, then turned and took Letta's hand to help her. As they continued to walk, he didn't take his hand away, and Letta was glad of the dry warmth of it.

Marlo stopped. Up ahead, Letta noticed the man had slowed down.

"Let's wait a minute," she said to Marlo. He immediately sank down among the ferns. Together they watched the man. They could just see him now that the darkness was beginning to fade. He had stopped walking and was looking around like a dog about to lie down.

"What's he doing?" Marlo asked, his voice little more than a whisper.

Letta shrugged and the man disappeared.

"What happened?" she said, frowning. "Where did he go?"

Marlo was already on his feet. "He's gone," he said, already walking toward the spot where the man had been.

Letta followed him. The dawn was just creeping onto the horizon. At the western end of the field they stopped. And then Letta saw it. She touched Marlo's arm.

"There. Look!" she said.

It was the entrance to a tunnel. A tunnel cut into the hill.

Marlo looked into it and looked back at Letta. "We don't know what's in there," he said. "It could be a dead end or a trap. He could be waiting for us."

"No," she said. "I don't think he saw us. He would have confronted us, I'm sure. I think we should see what's in there."

She hoped she sounded confident. Inside, she was quaking at the thought of what might await them in the tunnel.

Marlo looked down at her. "You're sure?" he said.

"I'm sure," she said and ducked her head into the grassy tunnel.

CHAPTER 15

NON-LIST

TAPE

PIECE OF PAPER WITH GLUE

After the first few strides, she couldn't see anything. The tunnel smelled of damp moss. It wasn't high enough to stand up in, so they walked along crouched over, stumbling on the uneven ground and peering into the semidarkness trying to see what lay ahead. They rounded a corner, and Letta could see light in the distance. They hurried on until the tunnel opened out into a clearing. Ahead of them was a set of high gates and a barbed-wire fence. Dawn had broken, and the early morning sun was spilling dappled light on the scene, glinting off the metal gates. Beyond the gates was a long, low building painted a murky color that soaked up all the light. The roof was covered in bleached-out slates that had once been black. There were no people to be seen. Something was not right here. She glanced around, trying to see why the place felt sinister. And then she realized. There was total silence. No animals, no birds. Nothing.

"What is this place?" Marlo said softly.

Letta shook her head.

Marlo pulled her arm. "Let's go back into the tunnel," he said. "They could see us here."

From the tunnel they watched the gates. Letta tensed. Someone was coming across the yard beyond the fence. A gavver. She could see his uniform now. In each hand he held a white plastic container. She squeezed Marlo's hand.

"He can't see us." Marlo whispered the words in her ear. She nodded. The gavver opened the gate and walked toward them. Letta couldn't breathe. Just as she was about to turn and run, he changed direction and disappeared into the surrounding scrub. A few minutes later, the man reemerged, the containers now appearing heavier.

"Water," Letta said. The man had obviously gone to a pipe somewhere nearby to fill the containers. As they watched, the gates closed behind him.

"We can't get over that fence," Marlo said.

Letta knew he was right. Was this it? Would they be foolish to stay any longer? The man and the wolf could appear at any minute.

The gate opened again, and the same gavver came out with two more empty containers. The gate didn't close behind him. As soon as he disappeared into the scrub, Letta grabbed

Marlo's hand. "Run!" she said, and without another thought she was out of the tunnel, chasing across the grass and through the gates. Once inside, she stopped for a second to get her bearings, then dashed to the side of the building, Marlo following her.

"Now what?" he said, looking down at her.

"Around the back," Letta said and ran to the gable. Rounding the corner, she stopped. "There are windows," she said. "Down there. I'll go look. You keep watch."

Letta kept close to the wall and edged her way toward the windows. She reached the first one and ducked under the sill. She looked around cautiously. Nothing. She pulled herself up and looked through the glass.

She saw a long and narrow room. Each wall was lined with small white cribs. A woman, dressed in white, was bending over one crib with her back to the window. Another woman pushed a cart on which sat rows and rows of bottles. Puzzled, Letta dropped down and moved to the next window. Again, she saw a long room, its walls lined with identical white cribs. Two more women were working here, going from crib to crib, their backs to the window. One of them bent down and picked up a child. Slowly, she turned with the child in her arms, and Letta's heart almost stopped beating. The woman's mouth was taped shut with heavy gray duct tape. Their eyes met.

"Leyla!" Letta gasped.

CHAPTER 16

#327

CHASE

TO FOLLOW, RUN AFTER

Leyla—Letta's aunt! The beloved aunt she had found among the Creators. Amelia's sister and Amelia's opposite in every way.

But Leyla was dead.

Letta stared at her, uncomprehending. It *was* Leyla, her long black hair tied back. Her beautiful brown eyes. As Letta watched, Leyla moved away and signaled to the other woman, her eyes wide in alarm. The second woman came to the glass. She was smaller than Leyla and almost totally bald. Letta opened her mouth to speak, but the woman signaled her to leave, her eyes wide and desperate. Letta shook her head. She would not go now. She could see the terror on Leyla's face. The other woman held up her hand… *Wait*, she seemed to say. Letta sank down under the sill. How could Leyla be here when the gavvers had executed her? Her mind went immediately to Finn. He had loved Leyla with all his heart. She had to tell him that Leyla was alive—and here.

It seemed like a long time before the bald woman appeared at the corner of the building. Letta watched her run across the grass, looking over her shoulder as she did so. As soon as she came into range, Letta pulled the woman down beside her. The woman tore the tape from her mouth. The skin underneath was scorched red.

"Who you?" the woman hissed, black eyes flashing. "What you doing here? They kill you if they find you."

"What is this place?" Letta said.

"They call it baby farm," the woman said. "Fifty babies here. Don't know where babies come from. No one allowed speak, no one." She looked around anxiously. "The babies must no hear words or they put to death. We put to death too. Amelia's orders. Tape on mouths"—she held it up for Letta to see—"to keep us reminded."

"But why?" Letta said. "What's the point?"

The woman sighed. "If babies no hear words, babies never speak. If you try teach them after first three years, they only able learn few hundred words at best. Nothing we can do. Us caretakers came from prisons. I not know what bring you here but, please, go! Before they see you. I must get back."

"No," Letta said, pulling the woman's arm. "I need to speak to Leyla."

"Leyla?"

"The woman who was with you in there"

"That not her name. Her name Yvette."

"Listen to me!" Letta said. "I know her. She is my aunt. Her name is Leyla. We thought she was dead."

The woman shook her head. "Gavvers found her on beach not far from here. They put her work with us. She not remember much. She been through bad times. They say her name Yvette."

"You have to get her to come out, to come with us. You too. Come away with us now."

The woman's eyes filled with tears. "No," she said. "No leave babies. No des-desert them."

Before Letta could say another word, the bald woman put the tape back over her mouth, turned, and hurried away.

Stunned, Letta hurried back to Marlo. "Leyla," she said. "Leyla is in there, Marlo."

His eyes popped like a startled rabbit's. "Leyla? Leyla is dead, Letta. Come. We have to go." He looked at her strangely, then grabbed her hand.

She pulled away. "She's in there, Marlo! We can't just leave."

"We have to. Come on. We'll talk about it outside."

Reluctantly, she followed him, her mind buzzing with questions. How could Leyla be there? She had to tell Finn. Marlo stopped at the gable wall of the building. They could see the gate, closed now and deserted. Marlo turned to Letta.

"We'll make a run for it. Hopefully we can open the gate when we get to it."

Letta nodded. There was no cover now. Racing across the yard, she tried not to think about who might be watching them. She looked over her shoulder. Nothing. The gate loomed ahead. She kept running, shadowing Marlo. When they got to the gate, Marlo grabbed the bolt and pulled. It moved easily. Letta looked back toward the building. Still nothing. Marlo took hold of the second bolt. *Come on!* Marlo tried the bolt, but this one didn't budge. He pulled on it again. Marlo thumped it with his fist.

Letta looked over her shoulder as Marlo hit it again. The wolf! He was standing at the gable. Behind him were his master and a gavver. For a second, they just stared at one another, they as shocked as she. Letta screamed a warning to Marlo. The gavver raised a whistle to his lips.

Marlo gave another tug. The bolt jerked. It jerked again and slid open.

"Go!" he roared at her, and then she was running and he was running with her. The air scorched her throat. A sharp pain stabbed at her side, but she hardly noticed. She tried to speed up but fear had its fingers in her back, pulling her, making her legs feel like lead. Behind her, she heard the whistle blowing. Clouds of disorienting thoughts scurried around her brain like mice. They had to hide. But where? Nothing but the scrub on every side and the tunnel ahead.

They tore into the tunnel. Running, running, though they couldn't stand up straight. Out the other side, Letta sneaked a look behind her in time to see two gavvers enter the tunnel. Each man had a dog, and out ahead of them were the man and his wolf. The wolf, slavering, straining on his leash. Letta and Marlo ran harder. Over fields, past the house, and back the way they had come.

She was afraid to look back now. The pain in her side stabbed and throbbed. Once again, she heard the whistle blow, the alarm raised. Once more, she was running faster than she had ever run, down a rutted woodland path. The original path they had taken with Edgeware was off to their right. Letta could hear the hunters gaining on them.

Within seconds, the ground grew softer. Letta felt her shoes sinking. She yanked her foot out and stopped running.

"What is it?" she gasped.

"Mud!" Marlo answered. "Water up ahead."

They pushed through the undergrowth and found themselves facing a vast swathe of rushes. Beyond the rushes Letta could hear water. Then she heard branches snapping behind her, barking. They had to get out of there. Within seconds, her shoes were full of freezing-wet mud. She pulled her bag higher on her body.

Below them, Letta saw the river. The bank was steep. Marlo plunged down without pause. He turned and looked at Letta for a second, and then she too started down. She sat on the wet bank and half slid, half pushed herself to the bottom, holding her bag above her head. The sticky mud clung to her clothes and her hair. The cold pierced her very bones. She was about to speak when Marlo held up his hand, warning her to be quiet. Letta listened. Their hunters were getting nearer—she could hear the wolf and the dogs baying, interspersed with the shouts of the men. She and Marlo sloshed through the freezing water of the river, while up above them the dark trees stared down as though watching their progress. Any moment now the animals could break through the trees and then…

As they rounded a bend in the river, she saw what Marlo had heard. A waterfall. The roaring of the falls might confuse the dogs. They hurried on. And then, with a sickening realization, Letta heard it. Barking, growling right above her. She looked up and saw him. No dog, but the wolf, teeth bared, eyes burning with excitement.

"The wolf," she gasped. "He's seen us."

Marlo turned sharply. Letta followed his gaze and saw the enormous animal trying to get down to them. She opened her mouth to scream, just as a cold hand grabbed her ankle and pulled her down. With a sickening lurch, she felt herself fall into the dark void below.

CHAPTER 17

NON-LIST

RAVINE

DEEP, NARROW VALLEY

It was dark, too dark to even imagine it was a real place. Letta squinted into the blackness and felt something heavy fall on top of her, quickly followed by a muffled groan, then more knees and elbows, until Letta understood that Marlo was there beside her. Immediately, a hand was clamped over her mouth, and a voice hissed in her ear. "Don't make a sound."

Edgeware! What was she doing here?

Letta took a deep breath, then another one, breathing in the smell of earth and water and moss. Her eyes were beginning to adjust. She could hear the wolf and raised voices. But where was she? Water thundered nearby, loud and insistent.

"Stay calm." Edgeware's voice came again. "You be in a cave behind the waterfall. The gavvers be right above us."

Letta felt someone take her hand. Marlo. She stood

completely still. Would the gavvers realize where they were? Beside her, she could hear Edgeware breathing. They waited.

Minute followed minute as the gavvers and the dogs searched outside. No one dared move, even though the incessant noise of the water covered most other sounds. The minutes became an hour and then another hour before they heard the gavvers moving farther along the riverbank.

Finally, Edgeware spoke. "Stay here," she said. "I'll see if they've gone."

Before anyone could object, the old woman had walked out through the waterfall. Letta could barely see anything in the gloom that surrounded her, but she could hear the wind growing wilder every minute. Thunder sounded in the distance and then lightning lit up Letta's environment, letting her see it for the first time. All around her, dark, wet stones leaned perilously against one another. Letta took in as much as she could before the light disappeared. The cold dampness clung to everything. She shivered.

Suddenly, she heard something behind her. She turned sharply. It was water. Water rushing toward her. Within minutes, it covered her ankles, her feet totally submerged. Where was it coming from? More minutes passed. The water was knee-high now and moving quickly. Letta could feel it propelling them toward the waterfall. She grabbed Marlo's hand, and they huddled together, pressing their bodies against the cold wall of the cave, but the water continued to rush in. Were they going to drown here? Marlo pulled her closer, and together they tried to walk away from the waterfall, pushing against the wild current. They were in a stone tunnel, she realized, that led up from the waterfall to the outside.

And still the water rushed on. It was like a bullet rushing inexorably to the waterfall. Its power was fierce. It was all Letta could do to stay standing. She clambered onto the rocks on her right-hand side, trying to stay above the flow of the water. They had to get out! Otherwise it would propel them into the waterfall itself. She tried to tell Marlo, but she knew he couldn't hear her. With one hand, she managed to get a fingerhold on a projecting rock and pulled herself forward. Then another. It was slow, tortuous work, but she pushed on. Marlo followed her. The water was freezing, and her teeth chattered with the cold. She had to keep going. She stumbled and just managed to right herself, clinging to the wall of wet rock. It was getting brighter. Was the flow of water easing? She saw a shape coming toward her. A human. The gavvers? She stopped. The shape came closer.

"Letta!"

It was Edgeware. The old woman reached out and caught her hand. Letta followed blindly, wading through the water. The pressure had eased. She could feel Marlo beside her. On and on they went till finally she could see light up ahead.

"Where are we?" Letta asked.

Edgeware frowned. "Nowhere yet. Safe place farther on."

Ten minutes later, they were climbing up out of the ground and onto a rocky path, an old dried-up riverbank. Great boulders were scattered carelessly on either side, and Edgeware used them for cover as they made their way onward and upward. Letta followed her, and Marlo brought up the rear. Every muscle in Letta's body was tense, ready to flee at a moment's notice. As they walked, they passed several small streams, bloated with water, the result of the recent heavy rain. Letta glanced behind her. No sign of gavvers or dogs. No sign of the wolf.

Edgeware beckoned to them. "This way," she said.

Letta wanted to stop and rest, but Edgeware pushed them on.

They walked all day, their shoes and clothes soaked, their limbs weary. Finally, they came to a field, and Edgeware stopped. Up ahead were trees. Edgeware moved off, picking up the pace again, and Letta could see she was anxious to get them out of the open and under the cover of the woods.

"No much farther," she said as they trudged on. "We be very near the rebel camp now. Hurry!"

Letta walked on, her body exhausted and freezing cold. But it was not her body that concerned her. Her thoughts were in turmoil. *Leyla.* Over and over, Letta said her aunt's name in her head. They had to go back for her. They couldn't leave her. She turned to see where Marlo was, and he waved her on. Within minutes, they reached a clearing, and Letta could see a sprawling copse of young birch ahead of them. As they reached the copse, it was clear that it concealed an enormous ravine, the edge of which was dotted with flares of light, while the facing flanks descended in waves of furrowed limestone like giant ribbons thrown carelessly on the landscape. The trail leading to the bottom was a slick of petrified barren ground, trampled clean in recent times. Black forests scowled on both sides of the canyon floor, listing toward one another in the moonlight. Below, through the trees, Letta could see the faint outline of tents huddled together, gray and vulnerable.

She tried to imagine the force of nature that had formed this place. Somewhere in the distance, a wild animal roared and she shivered. She looked back and saw Marlo at the lip of the gorge looking at her. Together, they climbed down, slowly, carefully, gray clinkers flying from beneath their feet in little showers. Along the sides, a network of vines and thornbushes straddled the path, marking the way. As they got nearer the base, Letta could see that the tents were long strips of gray canvas pulled over sticks and covered again with moss and other foliage. Scattered among them were the remnants of small fires, and she could smell woodsmoke on the night air. From the shadows, a man suddenly appeared.

"Edgeware?" he said with a smile.

Edgeware embraced him. "Rosco," she said.

He wanted to hate her. That was what she deserved. But he knew that his treacherous heart had always had feelings for her. Was it love? He wasn't sure. He didn't know what love felt like. Lying awake in the dead of night, he thought about nothing else but her. All those days when he'd seen her in Benjamin's shop, when he had given her water in the square. She had been playing games with him. The whole town knew that he wanted her for his mate, but she had pushed him away, teasing him. But that all changed. He would never forget the look in her eyes when he helped her escape from the Water Tower. It was then he realized that she also had feelings for him.

He took up the pen and began to write. It felt heavy in his hand, awkward.

"My dearest Letta," he wrote, and then he stopped. What should he say to her? What words should he use? She was the mistress of words. He didn't want to appear foolish or less educated in the old tongue than she was. He tried again.

My dearest Letta,

I think about you all the time. I think about your beautiful red hair and the way it caught the light as you walked across the square. I think about your voice in Mrs. Truckle's school when you spoke List but so cleverly, so beautifully. Even Mrs. Truckle was impressed.

We were always meant to be together. People said that to

me. I'm sure you felt the same. But you were always so busy doing your work with Benjamin. All that will change now, my love. When you come back to me, we will have no need for wordsmiths. No need for many words either.

He put down his pen. At last his life was improving. He was respected now in Ark, and soon, with Letta by his side, everything would be perfect.

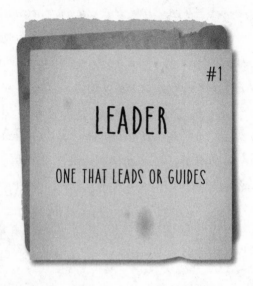

CHAPTER 18

#1

LEADER

ONE THAT LEADS OR GUIDES

The man nodded and beckoned them on. As they drew nearer, Letta could see people moving briskly between the fires, but there was a quietness around the place, as though people were waiting for something to happen.

They followed the man Edgeware had called Rosco to the site of an extinguished campfire, and he started to blow on the embers. Within seconds they had a fire. A young girl brought them dry clothes, and Letta quickly changed, glad to be rid of the wet rags she had been wearing. Later, the girl returned with hot soup and blankets. They ate hungrily, forgetting everything else for a few minutes.

As soon as she could, Letta drew Marlo aside. "We have to go back," she said. "Leyla was in that place, minding those children. She's had an accident and can't remember anything.

The woman I spoke to said that the gavvers found her on the beach. We have to rescue her, Marlo." The words were toppling out of her mouth, skittering over one another in her hurry to tell the story.

Marlo looked at her, his eyes piercing hers. "I don't know who you saw, Letta, but it wasn't Leyla. Leyla is dead. We know that."

Letta felt her temper flare, like a hot tongue of fire. "You don't know anything," she said, tears stinging her eyes. "I saw her. I saw Leyla. Do you think I'm a liar? Is that what you think?"

"I think you are mistaken," Marlo said.

She tried again. "Listen to me, Marlo. We never found her body. Don't you remember how upset Finn was? When he heard that they had killed her, all he wanted was to find her body, but he never did."

"I remember that, Letta," Marlo said, "and it wasn't unusual. A lot of people died and were thrown into the forest. We never found their bodies. It doesn't prove anything. We had people on the inside. They saw her die. They told us she was singing when they took her out." His voice broke. "And what about Amelia?"

"What about her?" Letta said.

"Wouldn't she know? She turned against Noa because he killed her sister. She couldn't save her. You told me that yourself."

Letta remembered. She remembered walking on the beach before the battle, talking to Amelia. Letta had tried to tell her that she had power, and Amelia had said, "What power? I couldn't save my own sister."

"He fooled her," Letta said. "He fooled Amelia. He fooled all of us. He didn't kill her."

Marlo sighed. "Why would he say he killed her if he didn't? What did he gain? Nothing. And it cost him Amelia. The woman he loved."

"Maybe he wanted Leyla to be a lesson to others, even Amelia. But then he couldn't go through with it. I know it's complicated, Marlo, but I saw her. I saw her. You have to believe me."

"I know you want to believe that, Letta. I have lost people. I know what it's like to wish them back. To turn back the clock and imagine what life would be like if they were still here. I lost my mother, my father, my brothers, my sister. I lost them all, and no amount of wishing will bring them back."

Letta steadied herself. She wanted to lash out at him, to punish him. "I lost my parents too, Marlo, and I lost Benjamin, and I never imagined that I saw them. I never wished so hard that I conjured them up. Believe me or don't, Marlo. I know what I saw. I promise you."

"And I promise you, Letta, Leyla is dead."

Without another word, he walked away.

Back in her tent, Letta couldn't stop thinking about the babies back in that place. They would grow up wordless. Trapped in their own heads, unable to communicate. How could Amelia be so cruel? Did she know that Leyla was there? Her own sister! What would Finn think when he heard? She had seen his distress firsthand, and her heart fluttered now imagining his reaction when he was reunited with Leyla. They loved each other so well. She tried to imagine a love like that.

Marlo's words haunted her. She had seen the way he looked at her. He didn't believe her. He didn't trust her. She couldn't bear the thought of them being on opposite sides. She was used to him being with her. He made her feel brave and strong. He always seemed to see the best in her, and that thought felt like a bruise on her heart. Could she have imagined it all? She thought back to when the woman had turned around and she had realized that it was Leyla. She hadn't imagined it. Leyla's eyes wide, panicked. It *was* Leyla. Letta was certain of it. No matter what happened, she would rescue her and the children. The thought had formed like a calcification, hard and unmoving. She couldn't turn her back on them. Everything else would have to wait. She reached out and found her bag. Carefully, she removed the card she had found in the wordsmith's shop.

Hope: to believe something can happen.

She repeated it to herself like a mantra, and she finally drifted toward sleep.

Later that night, in her dreams, she heard Leyla's voice singing softly, just as she had heard her in that prison cell.

Down in the valley,
The stream flows on
In the heather morning,
Quiet as a swan.

CHAPTER 19

#10

TIME

PASSING OF MINUTES,
DAYS, WEEKS, MONTHS,
YEARS, CENTURIES
EVENTS HAPPEN, ONE AFTER THE
OTHER, CAN NEVER BE TURNED BACK

The following morning, Letta woke early. The morning light bounced off the pots and pans neatly piled beside the fire. People moved around in a steady, determined way. Making food. Collecting wood. Talking together in little knots of humanity. She and Marlo were called to make their report to Rosco. They told him about the man and the wolf. They told him about the babies and the women who cared for them.

Through it all, Rosco listened intently, asking occasional questions but never showing what he felt. Letta watched him in turn. He was about forty, she guessed. Tall and sturdy with a well-scrubbed face and bright cornflower-blue eyes. His hair was gray and stood straight up on his head, giving him a permanently startled look. But it was his voice that made the greatest impression. It was dark and somber, as if it knew secrets that could never be told.

"We'll send some of our people there in a few days to see what's going on," he said. "If what you say is true, we'll rescue them. We've heard rumors of babies being taken."

"Can't you send people today?" Letta knew she sounded impatient, but she didn't care.

"No," Rosco said. "Our best crew is out on a mission. Now is not the right time."

"My aunt is one of the prisoners," Letta said. "Her name is Leyla. We have to get her out."

"One thing at a time," Rosco said gently. "We have to get them all out."

After their talk with Rosco, Letta went to help Edgeware, who was making dinner. The old woman was bent over the fire, using a whittled stick to stir the concoction in the pot. Letta could smell thyme.

"It smells good," she said.

"Spring is near," Edgeware said. "More green shoots. More life."

"Who are these people, Edgeware? I know you said they were rebels, but what do they do?"

"They move around. They be carrying out attacks in Ark. Even now…"

"Do they know Finn and the Creators?"

"They know them. Rosco and Finn fell out. They nay

agree on plans. Finn be going his way. Rosco come to the forest. All this time he be getting ready. Training soldiers. Making plans. Now he act."

It was one of the longest speeches Letta had ever heard the old woman make. "I told Rosco about the babies."

Edgeware sighed. "Amelia be carrying on Noa's work."

"If those babies never hear language," Letta said, "I'm guessing they will never speak."

Edgeware nodded. "People be afraid of words. Afraid of their power. But people be stronger. They will be winning out eventually."

"We have to save those children," Letta said.

"All the children," Edgeware said softly. "All the children, Letta. There be children in Ark too what need saving."

Letta thought of Thaddeus. His little face looking up at her. She couldn't walk away now. Amelia had to be stopped. Things had to change.

"You be a good person, Letta. A good leader. Ark needs leaders."

"Even ones who make mistakes?"

"We all make mistakes," Edgeware said. "But the greatest mistake be to stop trying."

Letta avoided Marlo for days on end. She couldn't bear to see the disappointment in his eyes.

It wasn't difficult to avoid him. There was always work for willing hands, and Letta busied herself hauling timber from the forest and keeping the fires stoked. It gave her time to think. She had been so sure she didn't want to lead anyone ever again. She didn't want to be the wordsmith. She wanted a quiet life. Let someone else change things, make the hard decisions. But now she realized she couldn't live with that. She couldn't leave those babies there. She couldn't abandon Leyla. She would do whatever it took, whatever she could offer, to end Amelia's rule.

One morning, a week after they had arrived, Letta went with some girls her own age to tend to the horses, ten beautiful creatures tethered to trees on the south side of the camp. They whinnied loudly as the girls approached, and they ate and drank hungrily. Letta stayed for a while, stroking the horses, enjoying their warmth and talking to them quietly. She had never tended to a horse before. Never been this close to one. Now she was in awe of their strength, the power in their sleek bodies. She would have liked to spend longer with them, but she followed the girls back to camp and went on with the chores.

She realized that it was a momentous day for the rebels. A mission had been carried out in Ark, and the soldiers were due back. She couldn't glean any more information. The girls were tight-lipped, suspicious of her. She thought of Carl and didn't blame them. Beds were prepared. A makeshift hospital was set up under Edgeware's direction. When the soldiers came back, everything would be in place.

Rosco took Letta to one side just after midday. "I hear you killed a gavver," he said.

Letta nodded.

"Two days ago, my men attacked the gavvers' base in Ark and blew up the living quarters."

Images of carnage filled Letta's brain. Bodies trapped in rubble.

"We killed over twenty of them."

Letta couldn't make herself answer. She couldn't think of any appropriate words.

"It's all-out war now," Rosco was saying. "We'll run a campaign of terror until we overcome them. We don't have enough people for an out-and-out assault, but the people of Ark will rise. With the right leadership—"

"Why are you telling me this?"

"We'd like you to join us. Help us."

"Have you heard anything about Finn and the others who were taken from the pump house?"

Rosco nodded. "They were imprisoned in the gavvers' base. We got them out."

Letta felt her heart surge. "They're out? Are they coming here?"

Rosco smiled. "They are out, and they are coming here. You haven't given me an answer. Will you stay with us?"

"Of course," Letta said. "Now that Finn is free, we can all work together, can't we?"

Rosco's face clouded over. "I don't know. That depends on Finn. Let's not jump our fences. He should be here by nightfall."

"Does Marlo know?"

"No. Tell him if you like."

Letta didn't need to be told twice.

She found him at a small stream north of the camp, washing clothes. "Marlo!" she cried. "It's good news."

After she'd told him everything, they sat together on a large boulder some distance from the camp.

"I'm sorry we quarreled," Marlo said. "I didn't mean to hurt you. I know that you believe you saw Leyla. I know that."

It wasn't what she wanted to hear, but she felt so happy that he was smiling at her again, that she could feel his warmth. Nonetheless, she had to ask him. "But you don't believe that I did?"

"Let's not talk about it anymore," Marlo said. "Today is a better day than I ever thought possible. We're going to see Finn."

He reached over and took her hand, and for a moment they said nothing. Letta glanced at his profile. How could any one person be so beautiful, so perfect? And not just on the outside. There was a force in him, she always felt, a force that was strong and pure.

"So Rosco rescued Finn and the others?" Marlo said now.

"Yes. Or at least his men did. Did you know Rosco as a child, Marlo?" she asked, remembering what Edgeware had said.

"No," Marlo said. "I don't think so."

"He knew Finn," Letta said. "I get the feeling they didn't get on. Rosco is planning a terror campaign. He won't stop at just blowing up the gavvers' base."

"Maybe that's why he and Finn didn't get on," Marlo said slowly. "Finn believes in being patient. Convincing the people that they could change things. He isn't a violent man."

"Will Finn help with the babies, do you think? We have to get them out of there, Marlo."

"So you're not giving up the fight just yet?" Marlo said, and Letta saw the smile on his lips and in his eyes.

"No," she said. "Not just yet."

"Please don't mention Leyla to him, Letta," Marlo said softly.

"Don't tell Finn?"

Marlo looked at her. "I don't think he could cope with that. Not after all he's been through."

"Don't you think he deserves to know?"

"Wait until Rosco sends his scouts. We'll go with them. You can point her out to me. Just don't involve Finn until we're sure. Please."

"All right," Letta said slowly. "I won't say anything."

"You promise?"

"I promise."

Letta didn't say any more, but Marlo's words played in her head all evening.

When darkness fell, Letta sat beside Marlo at the fire,

shoulder to shoulder, eating the thick stew that had been made earlier that day. Up above them, people were lighting the circle of torches at the top of the ravine that would keep the animals away. Letta felt her body relax, the warmth from the fire and Marlo's even breathing lulling her, and for the first time in days she felt almost happy. Across from them, on the far side of the fire, a young girl started to sing a soft, sad song, her voice like liquid honey, the sounds of the night fading away as she sang. As the last note melted into the night air, Letta felt as though the world had stopped turning.

"Wait!" Edgeware's voice snapped in the silence. "I hear something."

Letta pulled away from Marlo. Horses. She could hear it now herself. Blood pounded in her ears. Had the gavvers found them? She tried to see the lip of the gorge, but it was too far away. The darkness concealed it totally. She strained to hear the dogs baying. Nothing. Rosco was already moving, grappling up the steep sides of the ravine. Letta watched him, her skin prickling, her legs poised to run. She clutched Marlo's hand. After what seemed like an eternity, Rosco reappeared, his gray hair wet with sweat, his eyes black in the light of the fire.

"All clear," he said.

CHAPTER 20

NON-LIST

THINK

(1) TO USE POWER OF MIND
(2) TO HAVE OPINION

Letta could hardly believe she was about to see Finn again. Finn, Eithne, Carmina, and all the others. Images of the night they were paraded up the street flooded back. Carmina falling. Finn carrying her. On dark nights, Letta had allowed herself to think the worst. To imagine that she would never see them again.

She strained to catch a glimpse of them now as the horses approached. She had to swallow hard to stop herself from crying out with relief when they finally appeared. Two horses stumbling along, followed by four more. As they drew nearer, she could smell the sweat from the animals and see the plumes of fog hanging around their faces. A large man dismounted the first horse, his face wreathed in shadows, his body heavy and cumbersome.

"Marlo!" he shouted.

Letta was all but knocked off her feet as the man ran toward Marlo.

"Finn!" Marlo's voice split the night. A sob caught in his throat. The two men threw themselves on each other.

More horses arrived over the next hour, carrying mostly Rosco's soldiers. Some of the soldiers were injured, and Letta helped Edgeware clean wounds, apply balms, and bandage them up. The soldiers were quiet and patient, submitting to whatever needed to be done. Letta was constantly looking for people from the pump house. Carmina wasn't there, but she met others, including Eithne. She was chalk-faced, sunken-eyed, her clothes hanging from her bones. Letta tried to talk to her, but Edgeware stopped her.

"Let her rest," she said. "Be plenty time for talk. She be exhausted."

And so Letta helped Edgeware remove Eithne's clothes and put salve on the bruises and cuts that covered her poor body. All the while, Eithne's dark, watery eyes looked up at her from reddened lids, spent, lifeless. They were the eyes of someone who had seen too much, Letta thought.

One of Rosco's men told her that some of the Creators were traveling on foot. They didn't have enough horses to go around. Those who were able had walked. Some of the men would take fresh horses and go back to look for the walkers. Given how many were wounded, Letta wondered how long they could last in the unforgiving environment of the forest. She hadn't much time to dwell on such things, however, as Edgeware kept her busy.

"Take the oak bark, and mix it with the honey," the old woman instructed her. "It be a natural antiseptic. I need to make a tincture of mullein leaf for pain. It be a long night yet."

Letta did as she was told. As she beat the oak bark in a wooden bowl, her mind was with Benjamin. She remembered the smell of honey that had surrounded him as he lay dying. Remembered Edgeware's love and attention. She was glad that the old woman was here to care for these people and glad to help in whatever way she could.

It was almost dawn before Letta got to talk to Finn. He had come into the makeshift hospital Edgeware had set up to check on the patients. Letta watched him go from bed to bed, talking to the men and women who were injured, encouraging them, laughing with them.

She sat down on a bench near the entrance to wait for him. When he finished his rounds, he sat beside her.

"It's so good to see you," she said. "We've been so worried."

Letta thought his eyes had gotten bigger since she last saw him, but then realized that it was his face that had gotten thinner.

"It's good to be here," Finn replied, squeezing her hand. "We were worried about you too."

"We saw you that night. The night they took you."

"You were in Ark?"

"I didn't get a chance to tell you how sorry I was," Letta rushed on. "I know I was the one who put Marlo's life in danger. He followed me that night. He was trying to protect me." The words were coming in torrents now, and she couldn't stop them. "And that's not everything. I told Carl where I was headed that night. I trusted him. It's because of me that he was in the pump house, Finn. Don't you remember? I persuaded you to let him come—"

Finn caught her hands and held them.

"Stop now, Letta," he said. "That's all in the past. If you had not gone into Ark that night, you and Marlo would have been arrested. And as for Carl, he was my mistake."

Letta saw his features harden as he spoke. She desperately wanted to tell him about Leyla. The words were lodged in her heart like daggers, but she had promised Marlo not to say anything.

Finn was talking about Carmina and the others and how they had endured so much. He was worried that they might not make it to the camp safely. Letta tried to listen to him, but she was distracted by images of Leyla. She tried to imagine his face when he heard the news. Tried to imagine how his life would change forever.

"How are things in Ark?" she managed to say.

"Terrible," Finn replied, looking at his hands. "Everyone is terrified. After we were arrested, they searched every house, every room. People burned evidence or hid it, but the gavvers found plenty. The prisons are full to overflowing, and many people have been banished."

"Where do we go from here?" Letta said. "How are we going to make things right?"

"All the groundwork we did seems to have been lost," Finn said. "The people were just gaining confidence. I think they saw that they had a future. I really believe they would have demanded change, but now…"

"Rosco has a different plan," Letta said. "You know him from before, don't you?"

"I do," Finn said. "He's a good man, but he has a different vision."

"Do you think you can work with him?"

"I don't know," Finn said. "But I will listen to what he has to say. I owe him that."

"Who do you owe?" Rosco's voice cut across them, his hand clamping down on Finn's shoulder.

Finn smiled. "You, as it happens!" he said. "Except for you, I'd still be in that stinking cell where your men found me."

Rosco grinned. "You did look happy to see them, I've heard."

"I couldn't have been happier."

"Has Letta told you the latest?" Rosco's face was serious again, the bright-blue eyes sharp and focused.

"What's that?" Finn asked, and Letta felt her heart quicken.

"This baby place," Rosco said. "The gavvers have a group of babies in a building where they will never hear speech."

"The people who care for them have their mouths taped," Letta added.

Finn blanched. "Another language experiment?" he said.

"Looks like it," Rosco said. "We'll send a team there soon and see what they can discover."

Finn frowned. "We heard rumors of children being taken from Ark. I didn't pay it much heed," he said. "I should have listened."

"Is there no end to that woman's cruelty?" Rosco said. "Imagine taking infants out of their mothers' arms. Who does that?"

Finn shrugged. "Someone who has forgotten what it is to be human. I suppose she still believes that if people can't speak for themselves, they can't think for themselves either," he said. "While we were in prison, we refused to speak List at first."

"At first?" Rosco said, raising one eyebrow.

"For a while," Finn said. "Over time, we couldn't sustain it. Those gavvers are vicious."

There was silence for a minute while Letta imagined what they would have endured for their stubbornness. She remembered how they had tortured Benjamin.

"Less of them now, though," Rosco remarked, and it took Letta a second to realize that he was talking about the gavvers.

The gavvers they had blown up. "And Letta here managed to kill one all on her own," he said.

"Carver," Finn said. He looked at her, his eyes boring into her very soul.

"Yes," Letta said. "Though I didn't mean to kill him."

"Don't apologize," Rosco said. "He got what he had coming."

"I thought I shot him with a Black Angel."

Finn said nothing.

"I'll leave you," Rosco said, standing up. "I'm sure you're tired, Finn. Don't worry about the babies, Letta," he added. "As soon as the lads have had a rest, we'll send a party there. You'll be seeing your aunt before you know it."

Your aunt.

Letta could almost see the words fall from Rosco's mouth. Time moved in slow motion. She turned her head toward Finn. Waiting for the realization to dawn. Waiting to see the change in him. He looked up sharply. "Aunt?" he said, and his face and body froze. Nothing stirred.

Letta swallowed. The words lined up in her head. She opened her mouth. "Leyla," she said. "Leyla is alive, Finn."

CHAPTER 21

#430

UNIFORM

(1) THE SAME, NOT CHANGING
(2) CLOTHES WORN BY GAVVERS

The telling hadn't happened as she'd imagined it. Finn had taken her outside to a quiet spot behind one of the larger tents. There, she had told him all that had happened at the baby farm. She chose her words carefully. She had to be accurate. His face never changed. He just listened, his head bowed, his hands interlocked. When she stopped to draw breath, the questions began. He got up and started to pace. *Describe her. What was she wearing? Her hair? Who else saw her? Where did the gavvers find her?*

Letta answered carefully, patiently, but the questions were relentless. Finally, he stopped. He stared at the ground.

"Do you believe me?" Letta said. The words sat in the air between them. For a minute it seemed like he wouldn't answer. When he looked up, his face was haggard.

"I want to believe you," he said softly. "We were told that she was dead. Reliable people told me. There was no margin left for error or misunderstanding. May the Goddess forgive me, but I was thankful. I didn't want her tortured, starved, frightened. When they said she went to her death singing, I was proud. It was only afterward that I began to grieve. When I realized I would never see her again. Never laugh with her. Never hold her in my arms. It leaves you hollowed out, empty. There's a space you cannot fill." He paused. Slowly he raised his head and looked at Letta. "Do I believe you? Do I believe my lovely girl is alive? It doesn't matter what I believe. If there is even the smallest chance, I won't rest till I find her, Letta."

The sun dabbed a delicate indigo light onto his shoulders as he spoke. A white butterfly hovered just above his head. Letta remembered Edgeware's words—*White butterflies are the souls of the dead.*

She shivered. Finn had disturbed something in her. Something that had been lying quietly for the last years. The empty ache she felt when she thought about her parents, thought about Benjamin. In her head, it was a wild animal, and thinking about them was like poking it with a stick. It reared up now, raw and mean, and the pain she felt was almost unbearable. She missed them so badly.

She stood up shakily. "I need to sleep for a while," she said to Finn. "We can talk more later."

He looked at her, and she could see the concern in his

eyes. "I need to talk to Rosco," he said. "I have to go right away and find her."

Back in her tent, Letta tried to sleep but the day was just beginning to wake up. The tent walls went from dark gray to a lighter gray and then to pale yellow as the sun poured in. It felt like the world was beginning again. The harsh cold and wind had disappeared to be replaced with this far more hopeful sun bringing light and heat. Maybe their world had reached a turning point, Letta thought. Maybe their darkest days really were behind them. Hope bubbled inside her. If Finn could get his Leyla back, then surely all things were possible? She closed her eyes, letting the heat of the sun soak into her bones.

She didn't know how long she had slept, but when she woke, the light had changed to soft lilac and she could hear the birds singing. She got up and walked outside. The air was warmer than it had been all winter, and there was a feeling of spring. She inhaled deeply. Ahead of her, she could see a group of soldiers receiving instruction from Rosco. Curiosity moved her forward until she was standing on the edge of the group.

Rosco looked up and saw her. "Join us, Letta!" he said. "We're doing some hand-to-hand training. In fact, you can be my training partner."

He held out his hand to her, a smile playing around his mouth. She took his hand. Rosco pulled her toward him. He put his hands around her throat. She almost lost her breath. She kicked out, struggling to pull away from him, but his hold was like iron. She grabbed one of his arms with both of her hands and tried to drag it away, but he was too strong for her. She could feel the pressure of his fingers on her throat. She was about to panic when, suddenly, he released her. She fell back coughing, her eyes streaming.

"Use your fingers! That's what you should have done," he said.

She looked at him, totally confused.

He extended his first and second finger. "Keep the fingers rigid like this. Then jab them straight into your attacker's eyes. Want to try again?"

She didn't notice Marlo approaching until he was almost upon her. She knew from his gait, from the purposeful stride, that something wasn't right. He bore down on her with a face contorted with rage. She moved away from Rosco and went to meet him.

"How could you?" He spat the words at her. "You promised. You gave me your word. Are you happy now? Finn's ecstatic. He's convinced that Leyla is alive and they are going to live happily ever after. How could you? How could you do that to him, Letta?"

She had never seen such anger. His eyes blazed. Energy from his body crackled and snapped. It felt like a force field descending upon her.

She tried to explain. "Marlo! I didn't—"

"Don't lie to me. He told me everything. You make me

ill. You who talk about words and the responsibility they carry. But you throw them around carelessly, not caring who you hit, not caring who you damage. Didn't you think he had suffered enough? How do you think he'll feel when he discovers it's all a lie? Some kind of perverse wishful thinking on your part? Leyla is dead, Letta. And now Finn might as well be. He'll never recover from this, and you are the one who will have killed him. Remember those words! See what you can do with them."

But it wasn't the words that bothered her. It was the look in his eyes. She felt as though he had slapped her. Worse. She felt as though he hated her. She felt herself grow smaller. So small that she might no longer exist. She tried to speak but there was nothing there. Nothing to say.

Neither of them noticed Finn until he was right beside them. "Calm down, Marlo," he said, putting a hand on the boy's shoulder. "What's happened? Why are you quarreling?"

Letta opened her mouth but there were no words.

Marlo looked at Finn, his eyes dark gray like the bottom of a lake on a winter's day. When he spoke, his voice was calmer but hoarse, as if it hurt to utter each sound. "I'm sorry, Finn," he said. "I'm sorry you have had to suffer this false hope. But that is what it is…false. We got details—details about how Leyla died, details we kept from you. We didn't want to hurt you. We tried to protect you. There is no doubt in my mind. None. Leyla is dead."

"Then who did Letta see? We can't just leave things as they are, Marlo. If there is any chance that this is—"

"There is no chance!" Marlo shouted, the rage back in his eyes. "Why don't you see that?"

"I think you should leave us, Marlo," Finn said, and Letta could hear the steel in his voice. "I don't know what has made you behave like this, but I can't deal with it right now. I have to go and see this woman, and if it is Leyla, I have to bring her home."

All the anger seemed to drain out of Marlo. His face, which had been flushed, became pallid, almost ghostly. He didn't say another word, just turned on his heel and left.

"Don't worry," Finn said. "I'll talk to him later. I've been discussing things with Rosco. He doesn't want to send a team to the baby farm yet. He says it's not a priority. They've already sent a group on another mission to Ark. Rosco's blood is up. There will be no stopping him now."

Letta felt her heart stutter in her chest. They had to control Rosco. She couldn't countenance violence spiraling out of control. There had to be another way.

"I'm leaving tomorrow at first light," Finn said. For a moment Letta remembered the light that morning and the hope that she had felt. Now it had been smothered like a candle guttering at its end. She couldn't bear to think of the words Marlo had used—and she didn't need to. His anger clung to her like a web.

"I hoped you might come with me, Letta," Finn said. "Show me the way. Can you do that for me, child?"

She nodded numbly.

"Rosco has given us a horse. We should make it there in a day." He handed her some clothes. "Gavvers' uniforms. Rosco brought them back with him from the last raid. They will give us some cover."

Letta took the gavver's dull-brown uniform, the fabric harsh beneath her fingers.

CHAPTER 22

#473

TIDE

FLOWING OF SEA BACK
AND AWAY FROM LAND

It was almost dark when the last refugees from Ark arrived. They had been walking for days and were dehydrated and exhausted. Carmina was in their midst. Letta helped her to get comfortable, held a bottle while the other girl sipped water, and all the time they hardly said a word to each other. Carmina looked older. She had only been imprisoned for a short while, but she had lost weight, and her skin was dull and gray. Only her eyes hadn't lost their fire.

After Carmina had taken the water and eaten a little soup, Edgeware came to tend to her ankle, which was swollen and inflamed. As the old woman set to the task, Carmina caught Letta's eye.

"Marlo?" she said in a voice that was hoarse and bruised.

"I'll get him," Letta said.

She ran across the camp and found him tending to the horses. He looked up at her and went back to grooming the animal.

"Carmina is here." Letta said. "She's looking for you."

He dropped the brush he was holding and ran past her, heading for the hospital tent. How had things between them fallen apart so badly, so quickly? Marlo had been so certain that the woman she'd seen couldn't be Leyla. Could she have made a mistake? The hair. The eyes. It was Leyla. It had to be.

Letta made her way slowly back to Edgeware. She knew how busy the old woman would be with the new arrivals. How did she keep going? Her energy never faltered. Her hands were always moving: making salves, dressing wounds, cleaning and scrubbing. As she passed the entrance to the hospital tent, Letta looked in to see Marlo sitting beside Carmina's bed. Their heads were close together, and he was holding her hand. The tenderness he felt toward Carmina was so obvious that Letta felt a pang in her chest. She was losing him. If she had ever really possessed him. She couldn't imagine her life without him. He was her friend, her rock, her soul mate.

Someone touched her shoulder, and she turned to see Edgeware watching her.

"Things change, child," she said. "Let it go now and see if it come on back to you. The tide go out, and it come back in. Life is nay a straight line, Letta. It be a tornado. Don't try to tame it."

Letta listened and took it all in, but her heart was bruised, and as much as she wanted to make things right with Marlo, she didn't think she could.

She worked for a few more hours helping Edgeware and then retired to her tent. The night sped by, and despite herself, she slept. Before she knew it, she was dressed in the uniform of a gavver, standing beside a giant bay. The clothes fit Finn better. Letta had turned up the trousers, but the jacket still felt heavy and unwieldy on her slim frame. Finn was busily packing a burlap bag. She saw him put in a heavy bat. Two skeins of braided rope and a dagger followed the bat. Letta watched Finn in silence, trying not to think about having to use the contents of that bag. The horse was a beautiful nut-brown color, breathing mist from his splayed nostrils, standing patiently as Finn helped her up.

"Rosco could only afford to give us one horse," he explained. "But he's a big lad. He can manage two of us."

Finn climbed on, and Letta put her arms around his waist and held on tight. It took her a while to find the horse's rhythm, but when she did, she found she was able to keep her balance even as the horse picked his way up out of the ravine, sending shale flying as he walked. Finn pushed him on when the terrain allowed, but for much of the day the horse walked, winding in and out through the trees. There was still an air of menace in the forest, but Letta felt safer now she was dressed as a gavver, with a powerful horse under her and her arms wrapped around Finn.

At one point, they hit a road through the trees, and Finn let the horse gallop. His hooves tore up the soft, springy soil, sending it flying behind them. Letta clung to Finn, feeling the wind tug at her hair. She pressed her face into his jacket. Soon the road ended and they were back in the trees, the horse stepping carefully, the muffled thud of his hooves the only sound.

They didn't talk much, as Finn was concentrating on getting through the forest. They stopped for food and a drink of water after a few hours. When Letta tried to engage Finn in conversation, he seemed to withdraw into himself, and after a while she gave up trying. Every so often, they heard the cry of a wild animal, and at one point a pack of wolves passed close to them, chasing a fox. Their howls sent shivers running through her, but they were intent on their prey and ignored the two humans on horseback.

Finally, as the light began to fade, Letta saw the tunnel. The one she and Marlo had run through. On the other side, she knew, was the baby farm.

Finn pulled the horse up and jumped down, his bag swinging from his shoulder. "This is it?"

"Through the tunnel," Letta explained, her heart hammering at the thought of being back there.

"I'll secure the horse in the woods," he said and disappeared back into the trees. Letta stood looking at the tunnel. There was no sign of any human life, no sound. She wondered if they would see Leyla, and if they did, how they would get her out. If they were caught, they had no cover story. What could they say? That they were lost? And there was every possibility that the gavvers would recognize her. There was a price on her head, after all. She was the girl who had killed John Noa. She was the girl who had murdered a gavver.

Finn suddenly appeared beside her. "Are we ready?"

Letta nodded, though she didn't feel ready at all. In the tunnel, she kept her head down, smelling again the mossy, grassy scent, and then she found herself outside again. In front of them was the wall she remembered and the high gates. To their right was a small copse, and it was there Finn headed. Letta followed him, never taking her eyes off the gate.

They settled down to watch. Letta hadn't had much chance to examine the compound when she had been there with Marlo. Now she could see that it was quite a large area surrounded by a stone wall. The stones seemed to have been culled from somewhere else, with chunks of mortar still attached. The double gates were made from twisted black iron bars fashioned to look as menacing as possible. They were six feet high, hung on two stone pillars, unflinching in their job of keeping people in and keeping people out. Inside the wall was the long, low building that held the babies, and behind that were assorted huts where she imagined the staff slept.

She crouched down, checking the ground carefully, wary of snakes. Beside her, Finn stood in the shadow of the trees.

She could feel the tension emanating from him. He pulled out a bottle of water and handed it to her. Looking at the long, low building again, her thoughts were filled with the babies. She remembered how upset Thaddeus had been that a neighbor's child had been taken. Did the mothers have any idea where their children were? These babies were growing up in utter silence, not because they had to, but because someone had decided that they should. Not alone were their mothers' voices silenced, but all voices. The only sound they would hear was their own crying, their own babbling. Their brains would lose the ability to pick up language if they were left in that state for much longer—but that, of course, was what her aunt, Amelia, wanted.

Even though Letta had been upset listening to the accounts of the bombing in Ark when the gavvers had been killed, even though she didn't agree with violence, this act of cruelty needed to be punished. No one had the right to destroy these children's potential. No one. And what of Leyla and the other carers? She knew how distressed they must be. Cruel tape covering their mouths, smothering the words of comfort they wanted to bring. She could barely cope with imagining it.

Beside her, Finn stirred. "All quiet," he said.

Her eyes scanned the compound, and then she thought she saw something move. She reached up and touched Finn's hand in warning. He crouched down beside her immediately. She pointed. Two men had just come out of one of the huts and were making their way to the gates. They both carried steel buckets. As they watched, the men struggled with the bolts for a minute, then slipped through the gates. Finn took the knife from his bag. Letta's heart beat a rapid tattoo against her ribs. The gavvers were still walking in their direction. Letta didn't move. She could just hear their voices, low and hushed.

"Sleep tonight," one said.

"No on duty?"

"No. No duty tonight. Duty last night. Sleep now."

It was so strange to hear the broken cadences of List again. The struggle to smother the words you wanted to say. How had she ever thought it was acceptable?

The men passed within twenty paces, and Letta saw them disappear behind two large fir trees. Minutes later they came back with buckets full of water. She didn't move until they were safely through the gates and gone.

"That was close," Finn said, putting the knife away. "There must be a water source there."

They stayed another hour, watching and waiting, but nothing stirred.

"Let's have a look around the back," Letta said, relieved to be able to stand up. Finn followed her. The light was all but gone, yet it felt reckless breaking cover as they scurried across to the perimeter wall. Keeping close to the wall, they made their way slowly to the rear of the enclosure. Here the vegetation was more overgrown and it was easier to hide. At the rear of the compound there was another barred gate that allowed them to see into the yard beyond. They were looking at the huts now, a string of rough wooden structures, totally unlike the houses in Ark. These had been thrown up to give shelter and little else. Each hut had a front door and no windows. The ground around and even between the huts had been cultivated, and some sort of vegetable grew in the raised beds, green leaves waving in the wind.

They didn't have long to wait before they saw movement. This time, a young woman with blond hair came out of the babies' building. Her hair was tied back, her mouth was taped, and she walked with an odd gait, her feet dragging through the red dust. Everything about her said she didn't want to be there, Letta thought. The woman headed toward the huts. She swung her shoulders around, revealing a pannier strapped to her back. She took it from her body and put it on the ground. She dropped to her knees, and Letta could see she was pulling something from the ground. The woman slowly filled the pannier and was standing up again when the two gavvers appeared beside her. Letta couldn't hear what they said, but she saw the woman cower in front of them. They pointed to the babies' building, and the woman walked back the way she had come as the men stood watching.

Another hour passed. There seemed to be a low presence of gavvers at the compound. They didn't need them, Letta reasoned. Even if the women could walk out, where would they go? An image of the wolf pack they had seen flashed in her brain. The forest meant death, and they knew that.

Letta was cold, and her muscles were stiff from being in the same place for so long. It was totally dark now, with a slice of a moon lying on its back in a cloudless sky. The only sounds were the hum of the windmills behind the huts and odd animal sounds somewhere in the distance. Letta could feel her eyes closing, tiredness rippling through her in waves.

"Let's go back to the front gate," Finn said. "There's nothing happening here."

They made their way back around the perimeter fence and hid once more in the brush opposite the gate. They were just settled when Letta felt Finn tense. The door of the hut nearest to them opened. Two gavvers walked out.

"The night watch," Finn whispered to her. He pulled the bat from his bag. She saw him tighten his grip on the polished handle. The gavvers walked toward them, heads close together, talking. One of them held a tin bucket in his hand.

Letta crouched low, watching their progress across the yard. One was tall and lanky, the other smaller. They came to the gate and pulled the bolts across, the noise splitting the silence. Finn signaled to Letta to move away.

She scuttled backward, making sure to stay in the shadows. She saw Finn move stealthily, taking up position behind a tall oak tree. The gavvers walked past her, so close she could have reached out and touched them. She looked over to where Finn was hiding. In a second, he was upon them. She saw him lift the bat. He struck the taller one, the bat coming down hard and fast. She heard the dull thud as it made contact with the man's skull. His knees buckled.

Before the second man could react, Finn swung the bat again but this time, to Letta's horror, the gavver dodged it. She heard the smack of the gavver's fist against Finn's jaw, and then they were wrestling for the bat. Then Letta saw the first gavver move. Slowly, he managed to get to his knees. Letta saw him pull something from his belt. A knife? She didn't wait to find out. She jumped up and started to run toward them. She had to warn Finn, help him.

The gavver who had been on the ground staggered as he got to his feet. He hadn't seen her. She ran faster and threw herself onto his back. She wrapped one arm around his throat. He roared like an angry bear. *Hang on!* she told herself. *Just hang on.* She could smell his sweat, feel the rough uniform and the strength beneath it. He spun her around like a demented animal, trying to shake her off. She tried to hold on, but the force was such that suddenly she was airborne, flying until her head hit the cold ground. The pain was excruciating. For a moment, she couldn't see, her vision blurred. And then the gavver was above her, knife in hand.

She couldn't let it end like this. She wasn't going to die in this awful place. She sprang to her feet and, remembering what Rosco had taught her, stabbed two fingers straight into the gavver's eyes. The man screamed, but in a second Finn's hand was over his mouth, smothering the sound. The second gavver lay prone on the ground, the bat finally having done its grisly work.

"Get the rope!" Finn hissed at her. She ran back to where they had left the bag, and within minutes both gavvers were securely tied. Finn and Letta bound the men's mouths with rough gags.

"Let's go in!" Letta whispered urgently. "The gates are open."

Together, she and Finn went back to the edge of the clearing and crouched down. The night was now at its deepest, but the stars above them were bright and the weather was calm. Letta heard a soft sound. When she looked up, a woman, silhouetted against the night sky, was walking out to the gate. Her mouth was taped. She stood there looking up at the stars, not moving.

There was something familiar about her, the way she tilted her head, the way her arms wrapped themselves around her body. Letta grasped Finn's arm, but he was already getting to his feet and heading for the gate. Letta followed him, her body crouched as though ducking from a blow. The woman started and went to retreat. In an instant, Letta realized that it was the gavvers' uniforms they wore that had frightened her. "Leyla," she said. "It's me, Letta. Don't be afraid."

Letta could see the woman's eyes now, large and startled, like someone swimming underwater. She glanced quickly over her shoulder. Then stared at them. Her hands were shaking.

Finn held out a hand to her. For a second, she didn't move. And then, with one last look over her shoulder, she took his hand and walked through. Suddenly they were all three running back to the shelter of the long grass.

Finn held her in front of him, his hands gripping her shoulders. In one swift action he pulled off the tape. The woman gasped. Letta stared at her, and even before Finn spoke, she had formed the same words in her brain.

"You're not Leyla," he said, and the words echoed in Letta's brain. *You are not Leyla.*

CHAPTER 23

NON-LIST

DREAM

(1) STRONG HOPE
(2) SERIES OF PICTURES, EVENTS
EXPERIENCED WHILE ASLEEP

Letta had never heard such pain put into four small words before. She wasn't Leyla. Letta could see that now. Up close, the shape of her face was slightly wrong, the lips fuller. But the likeness was uncanny. The woman turned toward her, her eyes like pools of dark water.

"Letta?" she said, and Letta saw tears slip down her cheeks.

Letta stared at her blankly. And then, like tumblers in a lock, things started to click into place. She knew who this woman was. She knew why she looked like Leyla. There had been three sisters: Amelia, Leyla, and her own…

She tried to say the word.

She tried to form it with her lips, but she couldn't.

It wouldn't be said.

And so she chose a different word, biting her lip to make the first sound. Letting it slip from her mouth, though she knew it would change everything. "Freya?"

The woman fell on Letta, clutching her in her arms as though she were no longer able to stand. "Letta," she said again, tears now flowing in rivers down her face.

Letta clung to her, feeling her bones through the thin fabric of her dress, smelling her smell, her hand combing her hair. She wanted to stay in that embrace forever. Never to leave her again. She couldn't cry. She was afraid to let go of the emotion growing inside her. It was like a part of herself had been taken away and was now returned. All the longing, all the waiting, ebbed up, pushing past her ribs and into her throat.

"Dada?" she managed to say and watched her mother slowly shake her head. What did that mean? She tried to read her mother's face, the fine lines like a map, the dark eyes peering back at her.

She was almost relieved when Finn spoke. "We have to go," he said. "We have to get away before they notice you are gone."

Letta had forgotten he was there. Now the guilt came rushing in. She had done exactly what Marlo had accused her of. She had given him hope and snatched it away. She caught his hand. "I am so sorry, Finn. I had no idea—"

He pulled her into a rough embrace. "I think I always knew, Letta," he said. "I just wanted to believe. You got your mother back tonight. What could be better than that? Leyla would have been so happy for you. Happy for you both."

A noise somewhere on the compound startled them, a high wailing. A baby.

Letta had never heard a sound like it. It was pure loneliness, a cry of desperation. And with that, the bubble they had been in was ruptured, and Letta felt herself fall back to cold reality. They had to get out of this place. They had to get help and rescue these children. Nothing else mattered.

The rest of their escape was a blur to Letta. Freya showed Finn where there was a horse they could take, a small gray, tied up in a stable concealed behind the compound. Finn and Letta got on their own horse and Freya took the gray, and suddenly they were galloping through the night. Letta hung on tight to Finn, but she couldn't stop looking back, checking that her mother was still there. They rode all night and rested for a while at dawn, then took off again, exhausted, hungry, and cold. Finally, the camp came into view. They thundered down the slope as people ran out to meet them. Letta jumped down and went straight to her mother, who was holding her horse and looking around anxiously. Letta took her hand. Finn stood looking at the small group that had come up to meet them. Letta saw Marlo stroll up and stop on the edge of the group. Beside him was Rosco, alert, waiting.

"Friends!" Finn said. "I went to find my wife, my Leyla, as some of you know. But my Leyla did not survive. Instead we found her sister, Freya, Letta's mother."

There was a small ripple through the crowd, excitement, delight. Finn continued. "Freya has been held captive at the baby farm. I hope you can make her welcome."

Rosco strode up through the group. He gripped Finn's arm. "I'm sorry you didn't find Leyla, Finn. Of course Freya can stay here. We mustn't forget that she is Amelia's sister. That may prove useful yet."

Letta felt as though someone had just taken the oxygen from the atmosphere. What did he mean by that? She noticed that he never looked at Freya. Never even glanced in her direction. She didn't get a chance to think any more as Edgeware appeared beside her and pulled her into an embrace.

Edgeware turned to Freya and took one of her hands and kissed it. "You be very welcome, Freya," she said. "Come now and rest."

Letta followed Edgeware and her mother down the hill and into Letta's tent. She glanced back at one stage and saw Finn and Rosco deep in conversation. It made her feel uneasy. Marlo was nowhere to be seen. She helped Edgeware make up a bed for Freya. They ate a small meal and Edgeware left them.

"How are you feeling?" Letta said to Freya as soon as the other woman was gone.

Freya smiled. "Strange," she said. "I've dreamed of this moment for so long, and now that it's here, I can't seem to take it in."

"I always thought I'd see you come across the sea in a tiny boat with a silver sail," Letta said. "You and Dada."

She let the word *Dada* sit in the air between them and waited.

"Oh, Letta. So much has happened." Freya sat on the bed.

"Can you tell me?" Letta moved in closer so that she was sitting on the floor with her hands on Freya's lap.

Freya nodded slowly. "Your father was a sailor," she said. "He was the one who taught me to sail. When John Noa settled Ark and when the worst of the disasters were over, people were sent from Ark to search for any other survivors. Jack and I went on many of those expeditions and never found anything or anyone. Because we were often away for long periods, we noticed the changes more when we came home. John and Amelia were becoming more entrenched, more obsessive. We argued with them. We didn't ever agree with the language laws, but then John reduced the words and banned music and art. Leyla broke away first. She couldn't understand the ban on music. She and Amelia had screaming matches about it. All to no avail. John Noa was not easily persuaded, and Amelia was totally in his thrall. Leyla left, and we heard she'd joined the Desecrators."

"We prefer to call ourselves the Creators," Letta said automatically.

"That is better," Freya said. "I can imagine our Leyla as a Creator."

Letta smiled, remembering that first time she'd seen Leyla on the roof of a shed playing saxophone for the workers.

"I hear John Noa is dead?" Freya asked.

"He is," Letta said. Then, quickly, almost embarrassed, she told her mother the story of the Water Tower, the battle, and the result of it.

Freya frowned. "It's not right," she said, "that children like you should have to be the ones to fight on the front line. That is my generation's responsibility. This is your time to benefit from our experience, to enjoy our protection. But it's you who are protecting us. That's not right, Letta, not natural." Her face creased into a frown. She took Letta's face gently between her hands. "But I am so proud of you, Letta, and your father would have been so proud."

"My father? Dada?"

Again, she could hardly say the words, but she needed to know.

Freya sighed, a long breath of resignation.

"As things got worse here, Jack and I wanted to find a better place for you. Your father still believed there were other communities out there. We confided in Benjamin that we were taking one more trip, a trip without Noa's permission. What we didn't tell him was that we intended to come back, collect you, and leave Ark forever. Benjamin was still loyal to John. We just told him it was one last fact-finding mission. We thought we'd be away from you for a month, two at most. Benjamin promised to care for you till we came back."

"And he did," Letta said gently. "He died a year ago."

"So many deaths," Freya said. "So many good people gone."

"Go on with your story," Letta said.

Freya sat up a little straighter. "We sailed for about three weeks and then we met heavy weather, the worst conditions you could imagine. For days, for weeks, we were swept along with the tide, not knowing where we were going, maps and charts lost, hallucinating from lack of water. I lost consciousness. When I came to, your father was gone."

She stopped talking, and Letta felt that she was there alongside her mother in that little boat. The shock of those words, the finality. He wasn't there.

"I wanted to die then. I wanted to let myself fall into the black water and join him wherever he had gone. But I couldn't. I had a child to think of. I knew Jack would have wanted me to live for you, Letta. And so I struggled on.

"A few hours later, I saw a boat. A small craft picked me up with two people on board, Tory and Ellen. I came to know them well. They took me to a small island where they lived. A place called Farlow."

"And that's where you've been?"

Freya nodded. "As soon as I recovered from the grief, I wanted to find you, my darling girl. But I was no sailor, not like Jack. I tried. Please believe me, I tried. I couldn't tell you the number of trips over the years that were started and then aborted. Ever since the Melting, the weather has been unpredictable. And we had no idea where Ark was. There were times when I felt that my friends on Farlow didn't believe there ever was a place called Ark. They lived a safe and pleasant life on the island. They had good, kind leaders, and people had a say in everything that happened. They couldn't imagine a place like Ark. Couldn't imagine a list of seven hundred words.

"I could have been happy there, but I had left most of my heart with you, sweet girl. I couldn't rest. Finally, a refugee washed up on our shores. Like me, he had come from Ark. He had charts. I made many attempts, and then last year I set out alone and managed to make it here. As I approached land, a bad storm blew up and ran the boat onto the rocks. I am told that I was found unconscious on the beach by gavvers. I was brought to the baby farm and put to work. By then, I had sustained a concussion and had memory loss. It took months before I could remember everything again."

"The day you saw me at the baby farm… You didn't remember me then?"

"It wasn't that I didn't remember you. I didn't recognize you. I left a tiny little girl and you were a young woman. I'm sorry, sweetheart. I didn't know you."

"I didn't know you either. I thought you were Leyla."

"Is she dead, Leyla?"

Letta could hear the tight fear in her mother's voice. She squeezed her hand. "She died last year, Mama. John Noa had her executed."

Tears filled Freya's eyes. "And Amelia? She just went along with it?"

"No, she didn't," Letta said. Whatever Amelia had done, she wouldn't see her blamed for Leyla's death. "She did her best to save her, but Noa killed her anyway."

Freya looked down at her hands with Letta's hand entwined in them. "What happened to John? How did he become such a monster?"

"I don't know," Letta said. "But now Amelia is carrying on his work. In some ways, Mama, she's worse than Noa."

"Amelia always loved John," Freya said softly. "She could see no wrong in him. When we washed up here destitute all those years ago, we were three sisters with nothing and no one. We had fled from earthquakes and floods and found Ark. We thought we had lost your father forever. It would be another year before he found Ark. John Noa took us in. He let us live in his own house. All of that because of you, I think. I was pregnant when we landed, and John insisted that I come to the big house and see a Green Warrior who would deliver the baby. When you were born, he was entranced by you. You were the symbol of a new beginning. The first green shoot. You lived in that house for three years. Over time, John fell in love with Amelia, and you know the rest."

Letta remembered Benjamin telling her the same story. "They swore Benjamin to secrecy," she said. "I was never to know that you were Amelia's sister, Leyla's sister."

"But you found out."

"I did. The first time I met Leyla, she was playing a

saxophone and singing. She reminded me of someone, though I didn't know who. She was singing a song, and when I admired it, she said that my mother used to sing it to me."

Freya stayed quiet for a second, and Letta could hear her breathing. Then slowly and softly she began to sing:

> *Down in the valley,*
> *The stream flows on*
> *In the heather morning,*
> *Quiet as a swan.*

#17

SOCK

COVERING FOR FOOT

T he next morning Letta went to Rosco to talk about rescu-
ing the babies.

"We can't leave them there," she said. "If they don't hear
language soon, they will never speak."

"I understand that, Letta," Rosco said. "But a mission as
sensitive as this has to be planned. We can't just rush in."

"Why not? We know where they are. We have enough
soldiers. Why don't we go there right now?"

Rosco sighed. "I will send scouts in a few days to get
the lay of the land. The gavvers know that Freya has escaped.
They will be on high alert now. We have to wait. Let things
settle."

Letta realized she had to accept that. She couldn't do it
on her own. Yet she couldn't stop thinking about them. Small,

helpless things torn from their mothers, their families. She couldn't bear to think about what the mothers and fathers had endured. And what would happen later? Those children would have a whole life ahead of them. A life where they couldn't communicate. The thought felt like a pain. The kind of pain that took your breath away.

She tried to keep busy. She helped Edgeware and talked to Freya. There was so much she wanted to know about her mother, but even that couldn't be rushed. She wasn't used to her yet. There was still an awkwardness between them. Freya was still a stranger.

Rosco sent scouts on the fifth day. As he suspected, security was far stricter than the night Freya was rescued. There were more gavvers, more patrols out from the baby farm and into the woods. Letta held her head in her hands. They had to do something. She pleaded with Finn and begged him to talk to Rosco, to put pressure on him.

"You have to be patient," Finn said. "Let's talk to Freya again about the layout. The more prepared we are, the greater our chance of success."

And so Letta had spent hours with Freya, drawing a detailed plan of the baby farm. She learned that the minders worked in twelve-hour shifts and the gavvers did likewise. She knew where the dining hall was, where the dorms were, and that some of the windows were unlocked. Letta spoke to Edgeware about how they would take the babies back to the camp and where they would sleep. Edgeware made sacks out of old clothes that would each carry two babies and could be strapped to a soldier's back. Extra tents were being organized to shelter the infants.

Yet still Rosco waited. Letta couldn't sleep, could barely eat, waiting for Rosco to give the word.

Finally, fifteen days after Freya's rescue, Rosco announced that he would lead a party to the baby farm the following morning.

"I'm coming with you," Letta said as soon as she heard.

"No, Letta," Freya said. "You are not a soldier. This is a dangerous mission."

But Letta pulled away from her and spoke directly to Rosco. "I found the farm. I helped Finn rescue Freya. I have the right to be there at the end."

"You can come," Rosco said. "But you will take no part in the fight. That is for my people. You stay at the back of the group and take cover when we attack. Is that clear?"

Letta nodded, her heart racing. Freya held her tightly and wished her luck.

"Thank you," Letta whispered and tried to ignore the fear she saw in her mother's eyes.

Finn and Marlo joined Rosco's people, and as soon as the dawn broke, they set off. Letta rode at the back. She could see Marlo out ahead between Finn and Rosco. She didn't know how he felt about her now. She only knew that she missed him.

Missed talking to him, confiding in him. She missed the feel of his cool hand in hers, the sweet smell of sage that seemed to emanate from his body.

The horses slowed. They were approaching the tunnel. She watched as the others dismounted and Finn showed them where to tie up the horses. They would go the rest of the way on foot. There was a palpable air of excitement now. The soldiers fell in behind Rosco. He put his hand up, and they entered the tunnel. Letta followed. She was almost through to the other side before she could see the fence. No sign of gavvers.

Rosco's soldiers fanned out on either side of the mouth of the tunnel. Hunched low, they quickly took cover in the scrubland. Letta paused at the mouth of the tunnel. Something was not right. She couldn't explain it. It was a feeling. An emptiness. She stared at the compound. The gate was open. Nothing moved. There were no guards, no sign of life at all.

"Finn!" she called out, and he was by her side in a heartbeat. "There's something wrong," she said.

And then she was running toward the gates. Behind her, she heard someone shout, but she didn't react. She kept running until she got to the building where the babies had been sleeping. She stopped at the window and stared in. Nothing. The place was deserted. Where were they?

She turned, frantic, and nearly ran into Marlo.

"They're gone," she said again. "They've taken them. What have they done with them?"

She set off running again around the back of the building across the yard to where the nurses slept. That building was also empty. She stopped, exhausted. They were too late. She would never forgive herself if the gavvers had hurt the babies, or worse.

She felt Marlo's hand on her shoulder. "We'll find them, Letta," he said softly. "We'll find them."

She turned toward him, wanting to believe him.

He took her hand and led her back toward the gate, where Rosco was standing. The soldiers were carrying out a thorough search, but in her heart, Letta knew they wouldn't find anything. She walked around the yard in a trance. Where were they? A dot of blue caught her eye. She saw something thrown under a windowsill, almost lost in a tangle of weeds. She went over and picked it up. It was a sock, she thought. And then she realized that it was a pair of socks folded together. A tiny pair of socks that someone had knitted and dyed blue. Letta stared at them, tears flooding her eyes. She saw Rosco walking toward her and hastily wiped away her tears.

"We were too late," Rosco said. "They've moved them on. But don't worry, Letta. We'll find them. It's not easy to hide that many babies."

Letta nodded. She felt like she didn't have the strength to talk.

"Let's go home," Marlo said.

Letta shoved the little socks into her pocket and took one last look at the baby farm. Then she followed him.

CHAPTER 25

#38

COLD

WITHOUT HEAT

That night, while Freya lay sleeping, Letta went up to the top of the ridge and sat looking up at the coal-black night sky. A moon, pale as milk, shone down on her, turning her clothes to silver. She put her arms around her body and hugged herself against the chill. So much had happened. So much had changed. She looked up at the moon floating at the edge of this world. She saw it as it was—a cold, barren place looking down on a ruined planet Earth. Earth that had once been beautiful, with green fields and indigo-blue rivers, animals and birds of every color. If the moon had thoughts, it wasn't sharing them, she thought. It just looked on in silence.

But she couldn't do that. She knew that now. She couldn't hover at the edge and look on in silence.

She looked up at the moon again. No. She wouldn't stand

by. She had to change things. Make things better. She had to stop things before they got worse. She knew that Freya wanted to wrap her up and take her on that small boat with a silver sail. She wanted to take her back to that place where people lived in freedom. And there was a part of her that wanted to go. The child in her wanted to go to Farlow and live in peace where everyone had an equal say, and people loved music and art and words of all colors. But whenever she considered it, she saw Thaddeus's face, heard the wail of the baby in the baby farm, and remembered what Edgeware had suffered. She couldn't just walk away.

And then there was Marlo. Whenever she thought about the future, her future, he was part of it. She blushed at the thought. Maybe he didn't feel like that about her. But that didn't change anything. It was how *she* felt.

Her thoughts went back to the baby farm. There was a time for Farlow and a time to fight. And this was a time to fight.

The next morning, Freya and Letta sat by the fire and ate their bread and soup. The camp had become almost intolerably busy. More soldiers had arrived during the night, having attacked more buildings in Ark earlier in the week. They had killed people. Not just gavvers, but ordinary innocent people. *Casualties of war*, Rosco said. All Letta could think about were the children. Were they also fair game as casualties of war? She knew Finn wasn't happy, but there was little he could do.

Even some of his own people agreed with Rosco. People like Carmina. Letta didn't know what Marlo thought. She hadn't spoken to him since getting back.

"I can't wait to get you out of here," Freya said, and Letta could see how excited her mother was at the prospect. "They have a school there now for youngsters like you," Freya went on. "You could study, Letta. Read books."

For the first time in her life, Letta thought that reading books wouldn't be enough for her, but she said nothing.

"And there are exhibitions of art and concerts. Oh, Letta, you will love it."

She didn't know how to explain to Freya that she had to stay there.

"I spoke to Finn," Freya was saying. "He thinks he can organize a boat for us. It might take a few weeks, but the minute it's organized, we can leave. Imagine, Letta, you will be free of this place."

But somehow it didn't sound like freedom. A life without Marlo, without her friends. A life where she had abandoned Ark. Did her mother not care about all the people trapped in Ark? Did she not care about the babies that she had helped look after? Letta was about to ask her when Finn came upon them.

"Can you excuse us for a minute, Letta? I need to talk to Freya."

Letta was glad to get away. She rambled over to where

the horses were tethered and found the bay who had taken them to the baby farm. She picked up the old bristle brush and started to groom him. When her wrist got tired, she walked into the trees to pick some herbs. She knelt down and was soon lost in the gentle, rhythmic work of picking the bright-green shoots. She was startled to hear voices. Rosco and one of his men. They were over by the horses, their voices carrying on the clear air.

"She is our trump card," Rosco said.

"You think Amelia will pay to get her back?"

"She's her sister. The way I heard it, she was fairly cut up when Noa killed Leyla."

"What would you ask for?"

"Everything. Total freedom. No more language laws. Government by election. The old ways. Democracy."

"And if she doesn't agree?"

Rosco laughed. A dry, humorless laugh. "If she doesn't agree, she can have her sister back, piece by small piece."

"That's a bit vicious," the other man said.

"This is war. Desperate times demand desperate deeds."

Letta didn't move. She felt numb. That was her mother they were talking about. She wanted to confront them there and then, but some inner voice quelled that thought. She needed to think things through.

She went back to the camp. Edgeware was tired, and Letta was glad to be able to take some work away from her. She crushed juniper berries, banging the hard fruit with a stone, the dark juice staining her fingers. She didn't notice Marlo until he was right beside her.

"Letta," he said.

She jumped. He was looking down at her, his eyes cloudy.

"I need to talk to you," he said. She put down the stone she was holding. "Why don't we go up to the top of the ridge? We'll have privacy there."

She nodded. He turned and started to walk away. She followed him. She had only gone about three strides when she heard a furor behind her. Rosco was calling her name. She turned. She could hardly bear to look at him after what she had overheard. Finn was with him and some of the other men. There was an air of excitement about them.

"Letta," Finn said. "We've had a message from Amelia."

"Amelia?"

"She wants to commence peace talks."

"That's good, isn't it?" Letta said, looking from one to the other. Did this mean they could go home? Could it be possible that there would be peace?

"It depends," Rosco said.

"On what?"

"On whether she's telling the truth. Maybe this is all a hoax. But one thing is clear—our campaign is forcing her to act. Maybe we should trigger a revolution now. Storm Ark. Get rid of her and her cronies once and for all."

"But if there is a chance that bloodshed could be avoided…" Finn said.

Letta looked at Rosco. "This isn't a time for war. Not when she's looking to talk."

Rosco smiled. A smile that had no warmth. "And when is the right time, Letta? Can you ever imagine a right time?"

"There's another problem," Finn said, his face creased, his eyes sharp. Letta looked at him, waiting. He swallowed hard, then touched her arm. "She will only talk with you, Letta."

He was exhausted. It had taken days to convince Amelia to go along with his plan. She didn't understand why they should ask for Letta, but Werber knew this was his last chance to bring her in. His heart quickened. If all went to plan, he would see her soon. And all would go to plan. Amelia had sent Letta an invitation she couldn't refuse. Not unless she wanted more people to die. And he knew she wouldn't want that. She was a gentle soul, as he was.

Would she still feel the same way about him? He was certain that she would. He had seen the look in her eyes when he had given her back her freedom in the Water Tower. There had been love there, he was sure of it. He wanted to hold her in his arms. He wanted to forgive her for all she had done. She had been corrupted by Marlo and his friends. The gavvers had briefed him fully. If she was truly sorry, he could forgive her. He would persuade Amelia to forgive her too. And she would be sorry. She had hated the Desecrators as much as he had. And John Noa had loved her, trusted her. When she came in, he would convince Amelia that she was on their side, that the Desecrators had held her against her will.

He still couldn't sleep. There were ghosts everywhere. Their fetid breath filled his room at night, their long nails scraping against the window. Some nights he thought that they were looking for Amelia. Other nights he was sure they had come for him.

CHAPTER 26

NON-LIST

PEACE

(1) FREE FROM WAR
(2) STATE OF CALM

Letta felt numb. She was aware of a silence as people watched her. It was as though time had stopped and they were waiting for her to start the clock again. Amelia. Why her? Why had she chosen her to talk to?

"She's not doing it." Letta heard her mother before she saw her. Freya pushed her way through the small crowd and caught Letta's hand. "Someone else can talk to my sister. This is not Letta's fight. She's not staying in Ark. Neither of us is. Let one of you men go. This is not a task for a child."

"I agree," Finn said. "It's too dangerous. For all we know, it's a trap. I'll go."

"Very well," Rosco said. "You go, Finn. We'll back you up. Let's sit down and write a response. We'll work out demands and a time frame."

"I think Amelia has given us a time frame," Finn said wryly. "She plans to start executing prisoners in three days if Letta isn't in Ark."

Letta felt horror bubble up inside her. Amelia was going to start killing innocent people. In retaliation, Rosco would kill more innocent people, maybe even Freya. She might have lost her father, but she knew she couldn't lose her mother again.

"Stop," she said. The word burst out of her mouth, its weight startling even her. "I'll go."

Freya grabbed her arm. "Letta," she said. "What are you saying? You can't go. You heard what Finn said. It could be a trick. How do you know she won't kill you the minute you set foot in Ark?"

"I don't," Letta said. "But I know she'll kill others if I don't."

The color seemed to drain from Freya's face. "Please, Letta," she said. "I've only just found you."

"I'm sorry, Mama," Letta said. "Nobody is sorrier than I am. But this is my job. I'm the wordsmith. I need to do this."

"Your job?" Freya sounded horrified. "What job? You're a child."

"I am young, Mama, but I am the wordsmith. Benjamin handed on the responsibility to me. I am the keeper of words. I know Amelia. I think it's better that we do what she asks."

"Even if it means losing your own life?"

"I think she wants peace, Mama. She's not well. She can't

see, and last time I saw her, she could hardly catch her breath. I think she's as tired of war as we are."

"Let's go, then," Rosco said, and Letta could hear the impatience in his voice. "We need to get organized."

Letta felt her mother's hand slip away from her arm.

"One thing," Letta said, holding Rosco's gaze. "Freya is not a pawn in this game. Not now. Not ever."

Rosco narrowed his eyes. "Of course," he said.

"She is not a casualty of your war, Rosco. Be very clear about that." She saw the color rise in his face. He knew exactly what she meant.

He shrugged. "Let's get to work," he said, but Letta knew she had won that particular battle.

"I'll go with her." Letta turned to see Carmina behind her. She still looked unwell, but there was a gritty determination on her face.

"We'll have to protect her," Carmina said. "I'd like to be on the detail that goes to Ark. If anyone can negotiate with Amelia, it's Letta. But she's no soldier."

There was a smile on Carmina's face as she said this, and Letta felt a rush of warmth toward her.

"Very well," Rosco said. "We'll send a whole battalion to protect her, including you, Carmina."

Marlo smiled at Letta, and for a second she forgot all her troubles.

The day flew for Letta after that. She helped draft the letter to Amelia, picking words carefully, dancing around them as though they were land mines. And in a way they were. Letta would go to Ark under heavy protection. She would stay in Benjamin's house while talks were carried out. She would be provided with food and water. Then Finn and Rosco talked to her about their demands.

She felt she understood clearly what she was to ask for—democracy. One person, one vote. When Letta looked at the words on the page, it looked so simple, so uncomplicated, but behind those four short words lay the weight of all their dreams. No restriction on language. Education for all. Amnesty for the rebels. In return, there would be no more attacks on Ark. In return, they would protect the planet as best they could. In return, they would work hard to grow and develop their community. Letta hoped it would be enough.

As they talked and planned, Marlo stayed at her side. Edgeware brought them food and occasional words of encouragement. All the weariness seemed to have left her, and Letta could see excitement in her eyes. Excitement and hope. Letta prayed she would not disappoint her.

"Don't forget the babies," Letta said now. "The first thing we want is to know where those children are and that they will be returned to their mothers."

Finn and Rosco murmured assent.

"When do we go?" Letta asked.

"Tomorrow," Finn said. "I'll take you myself, along with six of our best soldiers and Marlo."

"I'll take everyone else," Rosco said, "and move closer to Ark in case you run into any trouble. We've also started to organize in Ark itself. We have a hundred men there ready to fight if need be. Either way, this is our time. If talking doesn't work, we'll try action. And this time we'll be ready."

"Let's hope it doesn't come to that," Finn said softly.

Rosco didn't answer, but in Letta's head she could hear the words he'd said earlier. *When will be the right time?* He was a man with his finger on the trigger. It wouldn't take much for him to pull it.

The rest of the day was spent in preparation. It was late afternoon before Letta got a chance to speak to Freya.

"I'm sorry, Mama," she said. "I know you are disappointed."

"I'm worried, Letta. I'm not sure I trust Amelia. She already took Leyla from me. What would I do if anything happened to you?"

Letta saw the tears flooding her mother's eyes. "It's the way I've lived my life," Letta said. "Always in danger. Afraid of saying the wrong word, afraid of trusting the wrong person. It has to end. No one deserves to live like we live. You and Dada saw that. You went against John Noa. You wanted change."

Freya smiled. "You are so like your father. I told you before, Letta, I am so proud of you, and he would have been too. But as you get older, it's not so easy to be brave. You think too much, imagine too much. Youngsters like you don't do that. We didn't either when we were young. Talking to you over the last few days has made me feel ashamed. When I came back here, I only wanted to keep you safe. I felt I had contributed too much already to saving Ark. I'd lost Jack, our friends. We should try to save them all, Letta. Go with my blessing. I won't be far behind."

"Do you think you could settle in Ark, Mama? A new Ark? Or is your heart in Farlow?"

Freya smiled. "My heart is wherever you are, Letta. We can build a Farlow here. Change is always possible. It happens with or without us. I'd rather be the one making the change."

Letta felt her heart swell. Her mother was still a fighter. "If anything happens to me—" Letta began, but Freya touched her lips with her finger, stanching the flow of words.

"Nothing will happen to you, my darling girl," she said. "Nothing. I will be waiting for you when it's all over, and we'll start again. In a new Ark."

Letta couldn't speak. Her throat was tight, and her eyes were burning with unshed tears.

Later when night fell and the flares had been lit around the edge of the ravine, Letta managed to get away on her own. She climbed to the top of the slope and sat there trying to process all that had happened, lost in her own imaginings.

She never heard a thing until Marlo touched her on the shoulder. She looked up and saw the dark hair, the blue-gray eyes, and wanted to run away. She didn't think she could talk to him now. He sat beside her, his long legs stretched out in front of him. She pulled her own legs up and hugged her knees.

"I saw you admiring the moon," he said.

She didn't answer. She loved the sound of his voice. She always had.

"When I was little," he said, "I thought the moon took people away. Once, I asked my father where someone had gone, and he said, 'To the moon. Look up.' I did, and I saw that friendly cloud-painted face and I wasn't so frightened after that." He moved a bit closer to her. "Have you forgiven me yet?" he said, and she thought she heard a smile in his voice.

Her heart stammered. "You need to forgive *me*," she said.

"For being wrong about Leyla?"

She nodded.

"It wasn't your fault. Had I seen her, I would have made the same mistake. I overreacted. I was trying to protect Finn, but I saw him the day he rescued Freya. Finn doesn't need me to protect him. He has survived worse things, and he carries her with him all the time, his grief but his love too. I'm the one to blame, Letta, not you."

"Can you forgive me for nearly getting you killed the night in the shop? Can you forgive me for not letting you stay to help Finn and your friends?"

"Of course I forgive you. The truth is, I never blamed you."

She let those words sink in and felt a weight lifted from her.

"But let's not talk about it anymore," Marlo said. "You

got your mother back. That's all that matters now. There are so few good days that we should celebrate them any way we can."

"I love that moon," she said. "Don't you?"

She turned her head and met soft, warm lips on hers. She leaned in closer and pressed her mouth to his, his sage smell filling her senses. A buzz like electricity traveled down her spine. He pulled away but held her face between his hands.

"I think I may love you," he said, and Letta paused, wanting to drink in those words, to savor them.

"Say it again," she said.

He threw back his head and laughed, a big, warm sound that filled her with happiness. When had she last heard him laugh? "I love you," he said, and he kissed her again, slowly, his mouth a perfect fit for hers.

"I love you too," Letta said, and as she heard her own words, she knew she always had.

"I dream about you," Marlo said. "And in my dreams you are beautiful but not as beautiful as you are here tonight. I wish I could give you the whole world, Letta."

"You are my whole world," Letta said, and in that instant she knew that she meant it. This was the boy she wanted to spend every day and every night with from now till the end.

Marlo stroked her cheek with his thumb. "I think I loved you from that first day in the shop."

"You had a fever, though."

Marlo laughed. "Even so. You made my heart beat faster."

"And Carmina?" The words were out before she could take them back.

"Carmina?" Marlo said.

"Don't you and she... I mean, aren't you and she... I mean—"

Marlo kissed her again, stopping her halting sentences.

"There are many ways to love a person," he said. "Carmina and I grew up together. She's like a sister to me."

Letta felt relief flow through her, sweeping away the last of her reservations. She lay back, her head on his shoulder, watching a cloud pass along the face of the moon. She had her mother back. She had Marlo. What more could she ever ask for?

CHAPTER 27

NON-LIST

TRUST

TO BELIEVE, TO HOPE,
TO DEPEND ON

T he following morning, Letta put her thoughts in order. Negotiating with Amelia would require all her powers of persuasion, her very best words. And in the background would be Marlo's love. She knew that would be a huge comfort.

Edgeware came to see her before she left. "Remember, you nay do this on your own, Letta," she said. "Benjamin be here with you and all the souls of the dead. Ask them for help. Trust in your words. You be the one with right on your side, not Amelia. I be staying here and praying to the Goddess and all the ancestors for you."

She took Letta in her arms. Letta felt the fierce strength in that small body, and it gave her hope.

Saying goodbye to Freya was harder. Her mother held her close and stroked her hair. Then she held her by the shoulders and looked into her eyes. "What did you mean yesterday when you said I wasn't a pawn?"

"I'm worried about you here on your own," Letta said. "Rosco sees you as something of value because of your connection to Amelia. Don't trust him."

Freya smiled. "I have known lots of Roscos in my time, Letta. Don't worry about me. I can look after myself."

"I have to go, Mama. They're waiting for me. I'm sorry."

"Go safely, little one," Freya said. "I will join you soon."

She pulled away and hurried back to her tent, and Letta had to use all of her self-control not to follow her.

Later, riding behind Finn and Marlo and their small group of heavily armed soldiers, she focused only on Amelia. She remembered talking to her after Noa had killed Leyla. She admitted that she had helped Letta in the past, sending her an anonymous letter to reassure her that Benjamin was still alive. She had hated what Noa had done to Leyla. Her aunt was not all bad. How could she be? She was Leyla's sister, Freya's sister. How could their blood not run in her veins? Noa had corrupted her. Letta understood that. Hadn't she herself believed Noa for longer than she cared to think about? And now Amelia wanted peace. She must have seen the suffering she was causing the people, the children, the babies.

The journey to Ark seemed to go on forever. Letta felt her heart lift at the thought of seeing the town again. Despite all that had happened, it was home. After a day plodding their way through the forest, they made camp and settled down to sleep within a circle of fire. And through it all, Marlo's kiss ran through her mind, an endless loop, like a tune she couldn't forget.

The following day, they set off early. There was a renewed energy now and a muted excitement that even the horses seemed to share. Finally, just as Letta thought they would never see it, the familiar shape of the pump house loomed out of the mist.

Slowly, they dismounted. Marlo took Letta's hand, and she felt a secret thrill at his touch. Together they walked into the old vestibule. They waited as Finn opened the trapdoor, and one by one, they descended into what had been their refuge. Letta looked around. The place was transformed. They had heard from different sources how the gavvers had pulled it asunder, destroying everything in their path. But the reality still shocked Letta. She walked slowly across the floor, seeing artwork in ashes on the hand-painted tiles.

She went to the north wall where the portraits of the heroes had been. The portrait of Benjamin. The portrait of Leyla. The beautiful portraits Carmina had created. Now they lay in tatters, some parts still clinging to the wall, but mostly they were confetti on the floor.

"I can do them again."

The voice startled her. Carmina was standing behind her, looking at the devastation all around. "I can paint them all again," Carmina said. "And I will. Don't worry."

"I'm glad you came with us," Letta said, and was surprised to find that she meant it.

Carmina smiled. "We might not always have agreed on things, Letta, but I couldn't see you beaten up by Amelia and her friends."

Letta laughed. "We'll always need good soldiers, Carmina, and you are a good soldier."

"If this works out, we'll need wordsmiths even more," Carmina said softly.

Letta took one last look around. "Let's go," she said. "There's nothing we can do here. The sooner we talk to Amelia, the sooner things will improve."

The words came out strong and true because she knew in her heart that all that mattered now was the future. They could have all of this again and more, but they had to act.

She led the way out of the pump house and into the damp morning. The horses were tired and walked slowly toward the wall of the town.

They were stopped at the South Gate of Ark. The gate itself was open and flanked by half a dozen gavvers huddled together like a murder of wretched gray crows. The horses stopped. The gavvers took one look at them and fell back. The riders nudged the horses on and went through the gate. The sound of their hooves was like a warning, Letta thought.

As they passed along the streets, people stood at their doors and watched them. It was still early, and the workers weren't yet in the fields. Letta felt the heat of their eyes on her back. Mostly they watched in silence. Occasionally, a voice sang out, either cursing them or murmuring words of encouragement. Letta tried not to react to either. She had never felt so exposed. The gavvers could shoot them from the rooftops, from the open doors. They had no protection, and she knew it. She was the girl who had killed Noa. The girl who had killed Carver. Wouldn't they want to kill her?

They stopped at her old house and dismounted. One of Rosco's men took her horse and she, Finn, and Marlo went to the shop door. It was open. Rosco's men stayed outside on guard while Finn, Letta, and Marlo went through the door.

Once inside, they pulled the great bolts across and Letta leaned on the closed door.

"That was different," Marlo said with a smile.

"I felt like a fly about to be swatted." Finn said, taking off his coat and throwing it on one half of the counter, which had been hacked in two. Part of it lay mangled on the floor, bits of timber still clinging to the wound like small, sharp teeth. The floor itself was strewn with words. Small cards, so familiar to Letta, lay like leaves underfoot. It was as if a tornado had passed through the room, leaving nothing standing in its whirling madness. The white marble floor was cold beneath her feet, and for a second she saw Carver lying there, the blood pulsing from his chest.

She pushed the image away and followed the men

through to the back room, where they found bottles of water and three plates of food waiting for them. Beetroot stew. Bread and apples. This room had been restored to some kind of order. She went to her desk. Her pen, whittled from a piece of wood, was still there. She picked it up and felt the comfortable solidity of it between her fingers.

"What do we do now?" Marlo said softly.

"Wait to be summoned, I suppose," Finn said.

Like we always do, Letta thought wryly. *Wait to be told what to do, what to say, what to think.*

"No," she said. "We're not going to wait till she sees fit to call us. Let's eat our meal, and then we'll go up to Noa's house and demand to see her."

Finn laughed. A warm, deep laugh that took the chill out of the room. "Fighting talk," he said. "And you are right, Letta. No more dancing to their tune."

They finished their meal. Finn and Marlo chatted, but Letta was lost in her own thoughts. She remembered the day she had gone to Noa's house and he'd told her that Benjamin was dead.

"You are the wordsmith now," he'd said. "Are you ready for the challenge?"

It had taken her till now to know that she was ready.

They walked through the street and up the hill toward Noa's house. The others formed a human barrier around her. Finn in front, Marlo behind, Rosco's men and women on either side. As they walked, she could smell the meal being cooked at Central Kitchen. The sweet smell of onions and fresh bread. They walked past the tailor's house. His wife stood at the door. Her small eyes followed them, her lips thin and pursed. The tinsmith's shop was closed, but his buckets stood on the path, flashing in the sunlight as they always had.

Letta's hands clenched as they approached the Round House, the gavvers' base. The bottom windows were boarded up, and Letta thought she could smell smoke on the air. Rosco's work. In the yard a few children played, kicking a makeshift ball between them. Their young voices were incongruous beside the grim building. Letta imagined they were children of the gavvers waiting for their parents to finish work.

At the front door there was a cluster of gavvers, statue-like, watching the street. Letta looked straight at them, determined not to be cowed. She had almost passed them when she felt something wet hit her cheek. Automatically, she put her hand to her face to feel a globule of spit, still warm. She stopped and wiped it away. One of the gavvers smiled.

Marlo put his hand on her shoulder. "Walk on," he said. "Don't react."

They climbed the steps. When they reached the gate at the top, they stopped to catch their breath. Overhead a gull screeched, and Letta heard the wind rise, its howling like a shrill whistle at this height. Below them, Ark was spread out like a great patchwork quilt, gray and green and totally still.

Letta walked up to the door and knocked loudly. Her bodyguards hung back. The door opened, and Amelia stood there. Had she been waiting?

"Letta?" she said, her breath coming in short gasps. Letta noticed the pale blue of the skin around her mouth, the bloodshot eyes.

"Yes," she answered.

"Come in," Amelia said as though Letta called every day.

Letta followed her down the familiar long corridor, conscious of Finn and Marlo and the others right behind her. All was quiet except for the sound of Amelia's labored breathing and the sharp clip of the cane that she now carried as it struck the polished floor.

Halfway down the corridor Amelia stopped and opened a door. "I wish to speak to Letta alone," she said.

"That won't be possible," Finn said.

"Go in and see for yourself," Amelia said. "There is no one else here. I don't think you have anything to fear from a cripple such as myself."

Finn walked past her into the room. Letta watched him inspect it.

"It's fine, Finn," she said. "You'll be right outside the door."

He nodded. Amelia led her in and the door closed. Amelia sat down and waved Letta to a chair opposite her. "Well," she said. "I didn't think we would meet again."

"You said you wanted peace," Letta said. "That is the only reason I am here."

"Peace," Amelia said softly. "That's what John craved, you know. He always said he wanted a world where the lamb could lie down with the lion."

There was silence for a moment, and Letta could hear the painful wheezing of Amelia's lungs, hungry for air.

"The time has come to acknowledge defeat," Amelia said. "Our experiment has failed. I think I knew that the day John died, but I was desperate to salvage something. Now I have come to realize that I am a dying woman. The Green Warriors have told me that I will not live for much longer. My organs are failing. My sight is gone. I want to put my affairs in order."

Despite herself, Letta felt a pinch in her heart. Amelia looked so unwell and so sad.

"So, what do you want, Letta?"

Letta thought quickly. "We know about your latest experiment," she said, not disguising the disgust she felt. "The baby farm."

Amelia nodded. Her expression never changed. Her eyes looked into the middle distance.

Letta pushed on. "What have you done with them?"

"We had to move them for security reasons. They are quite safe."

"We want those babies returned to their mothers. There will be no negotiations until that is done."

She hadn't realized she was going to say that. The words had come unbidden almost, but now that she had said it, she knew that she meant it.

Amelia nodded again. "I will see to it," she said.

Letta didn't know whether to believe her or not.

"So what else do you want, Letta? You are not killing people just for that, I imagine?"

"Us killing people?" Letta said, anger flaring like a hot poker. "What about all the people you've killed, Amelia? What about Tin Town?"

Amelia shrugged. "We had to protect ourselves."

"From defenseless civilians and babies?"

She saw Amelia wince. "What do you want, Letta?" she said again.

"We want freedom," Letta said. "We want democracy and freedom of speech."

Amelia laughed a dry laugh that quickly became a bout of coughing. She reached for a glass of water and sipped it. "So you want democracy. You want to go back to the way things were because that worked out so well for all of us."

"Every system has its weaknesses, and the old system wasn't perfect. But it was better than this."

Amelia took another sip of water. "In the old days there was a lot of talk about freedom of speech," she said. "I grew to understand that it was free but not necessarily true. People made wild, baseless claims. They said there was no such thing as global warming! Or that people who didn't look like us didn't think like us! People were free to say whatever they liked, and so they did. And that's what you want back?"

"Yes," Letta said. "People have learned a lot from what happened. They aren't stupid. We can do better. We won't do it by taking babies from their mothers, though. Of that I am certain."

"I see," Amelia said and sighed. "I will think about what you have said. I think you had better leave now. I am tired."

"And the children? The babies?"

"I gave you my word, Letta. I will see to it."

"We can talk again tomorrow," Letta said and stood up. She headed for the door.

"Letta!" The voice stopped her in her tracks. She turned. "Change comes slowly. You may need to be patient."

Letta looked at her carefully. "I don't think either one of us has time for patience," she said.

As she walked through the door, she could hear Amelia gasping for air.

CHAPTER 28

8

TALK

TO USE SPOKEN WORDS,
NOT ALWAYS TRUTH

Back in her old home, Letta felt as though a weight had been lifted from her. Things were about to change forever. She sat at her old desk and allowed herself to dream about the future.

Later, eating their evening meal, she told Finn and Marlo all that had happened.

"So you think that she has acknowledged defeat?" Finn said.

"I really do," Letta said. "I mean, she's still arguing about the value of the old system, but she knows now that Noa's plan can never work."

"I find it hard to believe she's given up so easily," Marlo said.

"She's exhausted, Marlo. You saw her. She can barely breathe."

Marlo nodded, but Letta felt that he wasn't convinced. It was only natural, she thought. He'd been outside the system for so long, it would take time to build his trust.

"Rosco and his people have moved into the old pump house," Finn said. "I spoke to him this afternoon. Freya and Edgeware are with them. They are getting ready to do battle if need be."

Letta felt uneasy. "Isn't that a bit of an overreaction? We've just started peace talks, and he's getting ready for war?"

"Rosco never was a great believer in talk," Finn said with a smile. "He's just being careful, Letta."

"But what if the gavvers find out? How can I make Amelia trust me if behind her back we are planning a war?"

"We're not planning one," Marlo said, and Letta heard a new sharpness in his tone. "We're just buying some insurance."

She couldn't argue with that logic, but it didn't sit easily with her. Her gut told her that peace would only be brokered if there was trust on both sides. She said nothing more that night, and for the rest of the week, she went up and down to Amelia, each time under heavy escort, each time meeting in that room where she had first spoken to Noa. She began to look forward to those conversations with Amelia. They discussed education and art and music, and though Letta couldn't always convince Amelia to see things her way, she felt that she was making progress. But still the issue of the babies had not been resolved.

"It is a matter of administration," Amelia said. "We have

to go through our files and make sure the babies go back to the correct parents. It takes time."

"This is not negotiable," Letta said. "There have been too many delays already. The children need to get back to normal life. As it is, we don't know what damage has been done to them. If they don't hear language, they may never speak. There are enough wordless people in Ark, Amelia. Stop your experiment. Give them back."

Amelia sighed. "Another week. It should all be done by then."

A week later, Letta came to another meeting with Amelia, but this time there was someone else in the room.

"I think you know Werber," Amelia said. "He is a Green Warrior now and one of my most trusted advisers."

Werber. The last time she'd seen him, he'd saved her life at the Water Tower. She had known him since she was a child. He had wanted to take her as a mate. She'd known that for years. She'd never liked him.

"Werber," she said. "No harm."

"No harm," Werber replied, looking at her intently. "I think we should discuss the handover," he said.

She couldn't take her eyes off him. Something was different about him. It was the first time Letta had heard him speak anything but List, for one thing. He had always been arrogant, vain, but now he was full of a different kind of confidence.

"Amelia and I would like to make a proposal," he said.

Letta waited.

"This would be a temporary arrangement until we were ready to have an election."

"And what would the arrangement be?" Letta said.

Werber cleared his throat. "Amelia would like me to lead Ark on her behalf with one of your people. We would work side by side until the…the…transfer was complete."

"You?" She could barely conceal her astonishment. She saw his body stiffen.

"Yes, me. Why not me?"

Letta realized she had offended him and pressed on. "One of our people would have an equal role?" Could this really be happening? Would they hand over power so easily? "Finn," she said without hesitation. "If our people agree to the plan, I think Finn would be the one to represent us."

"Leyla's partner," Amelia said softly.

Letta nodded.

"I think we should move on this as quickly as possible," Werber said. "Amelia is not well, and this stress is only making her condition worse."

He had the same eager-to-please quality to his voice that Letta had always found annoying, as if he were already minimizing their challenges.

"I need to discuss your proposal with my people," Letta said.

"With the Desecrators?"

Letta could hear the sneer behind his words. "We prefer to be called Creators," she said.

Werber shrugged.

Amelia sighed. Her face was now whey-white, her eyes heavy and sagging, and the high room seemed to amplify her ragged breathing.

"Are you all right, Amelia?" Werber asked, going to her.

A bout of coughing consumed her, and Werber took a tincture from his pocket and pressed it to her lips. Amelia's body convulsed for a second, and she seemed to have stopped breathing altogether. Letta found she was holding her own breath, and then, like a dam breaking, the wheezing started again.

She stood up. "I should go," she said.

Werber nodded and went back to ministering to Amelia.

Letta fled. Her head was reeling. She couldn't wait to share the news with Marlo and Finn. As soon as they were inside the door of the shop, she told them.

"A power share?" Finn said, frowning.

"Only until we can hold an election," Letta said.

Marlo looked doubtful. "How do you feel about Werber? Do you think we can trust him?"

"When Noa was alive, Werber was totally devoted to him, but he still helped me to escape. Despite that, I've never liked him. He's too fawning. Always trying to please someone else."

"I've heard things," Marlo said. "Apparently he was

always a coward, but recently he seems to be falling apart. Turc, one of our undercover agents in the gavvers, told me that he's found him walking around at night muttering about the dead."

"What about the dead?" Finn asked.

Marlo shrugged. "He's afraid of them. Afraid the people they've killed will haunt him. He was heavily involved in the massacre at Tin Town."

"I hope they do haunt him," Letta said. "I really don't think he's anything to worry about. We'll be well able to handle him when the time comes. And anyway, after the election we need have no more to do with him. Can we get back to talking about the actual proposal now?"

They talked about it for hours, with Letta trying to persuade them that the merger was the best way to go.

"I think we should slow down," Marlo said. "This is all happening too fast. We don't know what we are agreeing to, and we still have no progress on the babies."

Letta felt her temper flare. "We do know what we are agreeing to! We are agreeing to peace. We can't keep holding back. They have all the cards. Amelia is dying. She said the babies will be returned by the end of this week. She wants to get this sorted before she dies."

Finn paced the floor. "We don't want to agree to anything until we've thought it through. The best solution would be a fresh start. No Werber. No one from that regime at all. That would be ideal."

"I know," Letta said. "I just don't know if we can have everything, Finn. I think we should take what is on offer and build on that. I can handle Werber. I know I can. Once we call an election, it will be a level playing field again."

Finn didn't look convinced.

Later that night, she lay in bed trying to sleep. She had to persuade Amelia to open the conversation to Finn and Marlo and maybe even Rosco. They couldn't go on hearing everything secondhand. She had to keep things moving forward. That was her last thought before sleep overcame her. She fell into the deep blackness and dreamed of Benjamin and white butterflies.

CHAPTER 29

NON-LIST

SECRET

KEEP FROM BEING SEEN
OR KNOWN BY OTHERS

I n the morning, Finn called her early.

"We've had a message from Amelia. She wants to meet today."

"But our arrangement was for tomorrow."

"I know," Finn said. "Something must have happened."

"I'll go," Letta said. "She wouldn't have sent for me without a good reason. It's probably to do with the release of the babies."

"We don't have all your bodyguards," Finn said. "They're back at the pump house with Rosco. They didn't expect to be needed today."

"If you and Marlo come with me, that will be enough. I think we've seen that she doesn't mean us any harm."

Marlo shrugged.

"I agree," Finn said. "It would be good to find out more about this power-sharing idea. But remember, Letta, ideally we don't want any truck with them. What Ark needs is a fresh start."

Letta nodded.

On the way to Noa's house, she saw the line of people heading to Central Kitchen. Letta's food was still delivered to her. Amelia obviously didn't want the Creators to mix with the ordinary people. It was one of the things she most hated about Ark now. This concept of "ordinary" people. In the new Ark, she told herself, no one would be ordinary or everyone would be ordinary.

A young girl opened the door of Noa's house.

"I need to speak to Amelia," Letta said.

The girl frowned and glanced behind her nervously. "She not well. She not able see anyone. You leave."

"It's all right, May." Werber's voice cut across the conversation before Letta could reply. "Please come in," he said. "I'm sure Amelia would be delighted to see you."

Letta marveled again at the smoothness of his language. There was no trace of List left in his perfectly crafted sentences. Finn and Marlo followed her through the door. They walked down the long corridor and stopped at the room they always used. Werber and Letta went through the door, and Finn and Marlo took up their positions outside. Werber closed the door.

"Amelia is through here," Werber said and strode across

the floor. Letta was confused. There was no other door in this room except the one that led outside onto the terrace. "She is very unwell, I'm afraid."

On the far wall there was a row of oak paneling. Letta watched as Werber pressed one of the panels. An opening appeared in the wall, and Letta could see light beyond it. Curious, she followed Werber through this new door into a small anteroom. Behind her, she heard Werber push the panel back into place.

"Wait here," he said and exited through a door opposite. The door snapped shut behind him, and Letta began to feel uneasy. What was she doing in here? Where was Amelia? She walked to the door that Werber had just closed. She turned the handle. It was locked. She looked around. No windows. No other doors. She went back to the paneling through which they had come. Nothing. No matter how desperately she searched, pressing and tapping on the wood, she couldn't make the secret door open. She felt the blood drain from her face. She was trapped. What was Werber up to?

At that very moment, two burly gavvers came through the door that Werber had left by and grabbed her roughly. Letta kicked out. She screamed but all to no avail. With two deft movements, they had secured her arms and covered her mouth with tape. Sweat poured down her face, blinding her, as they manhandled her through the door into a shadowy passageway and down a narrow flight of stairs, her feet barely touching the ground. The stairs led to another gloomy corridor, and suddenly Letta realized where she was. These were the holding cells beneath Noa's house. These were the cells where they had kept Leyla.

The gavvers stopped. In front of her, Letta could see a heavy wooden door. One of the gavvers pulled the bolts across. The door opened, and Letta felt a blast of cold air. There was a flight of steps leading up to the street above. This was the last thing Letta saw before one of the gavvers shoved a brown hemp sack over her head and she was plunged into darkness.

CHAPTER 30

NON-LIST

FORGIVE

TO LET GO OF ANGER,
TO EXCUSE

It was nighttime. Letta was sure of that. There was a strange hush all around her. The gavvers hurried her out of the building into the night air. She felt a light sprinkling of rain on her bare legs. She couldn't see anything inside the hood, and everything she heard was muffled. The gavvers gripped her upper arms and half dragged, half carried her down the steps from Noa's house. They didn't speak and they moved quickly. She was terrified they would let her fall. She guessed they were headed for the Round House, the gavvers' base. A voice in her head mocked her. Maybe this was the end. Maybe they were going to the forest, where they would shoot her and leave her body for the wolves.

Suddenly they stopped. She heard a key turn, a door open. They were inside again. Still no noise. Down a flight of stairs.

They stopped again. She heard the creaking wail of iron gates opening reluctantly, and a shove in the back sent her sprawling onto a cold, wet stone floor. The sack was removed. Then without a word, they left her. She tried to cry out, but the gag muffled every sound. Her hands were still tied behind her, and the binding ate into her skin. But it was the gag that worried her most. It was some kind of tape that smelled strongly of iodine and made her stomach turn. But worse than that, she wasn't sure if she could breathe properly with her mouth taped. She tried not to panic, but every breath was already hurting her. She willed herself to calm down. She tried to breathe slowly in and out through her nose, to ignore the sharp smell, control her thoughts. She used a trick she had tried before. She recited words to herself. The names of wild birds.

Robin, blackbird, thrush, cuckoo, eagle, sparrow.

Her breathing slowed. She tried to wriggle her mouth, to stretch her jaws to loosen the gag. She managed to make it feel less constricting, but the glue would never allow it to come off easily. Her thoughts turned to Finn and Marlo. Where were they? How had this happened? What was Amelia playing at? She had believed her. All that talk about the babies. It was all lies. There would be no power sharing. Amelia had fooled her. The shame Letta felt was like a hot poker.

She spent the rest of the night on the cold floor, water

collecting in puddles around her. When her eyes adjusted to the darkness, she saw a grate above her head. She knew where she was now. The cells under the Round House. She remembered the day she had gone there to contact Marlo and the Creators. Hugo, an old man, had been chained up in a cell just like this one, and she had squatted down and spoken to him through the grating. If Hugo could endure this, then so could she. She gritted her teeth and waited.

The gavvers returned at first light. The same two men pulled the tape from her mouth. She felt the tender skin on her lips tear. She opened her mouth and gulped in air. They undid the bonds from her hands and gave her water and dry bread. Still without a word, they left. She waited till they were gone to eat and drink. She gulped the cold water, holding it in her mouth before swallowing. The bread was coarse and dry, but it took the edge off the hunger that had begun to consume her. She looked around the cell. It was five strides in either direction. No window. Just the grating. She stood on tiptoe and looked out. All she could see was a rectangle of blue-black tar, the gavvers' yard. Apart from a chorus of squabbling gulls, it was quiet outside. Too early for many people to be up and about, she thought.

She heard a bell sound inside and guessed it was the changing of the shift. Sure enough, within minutes she saw a procession of black boots pass in front of the grating. Men, mostly, talking in low voices, tired after the night. She imagined the new shift arriving at the front door and the day starting again. There were more sounds now. Horses, voices, and the sound of children. She remembered seeing children in front of the gavvers' base before. She saw two sets of small feet approach the grating.

"Who you wait?" one said.

"Dada," the other replied.

"Go Central Kitchen?"

"No. Wait."

The other boy started to walk away. "See later?"

"Yes. Later," the remaining one said, and Letta's heart tripped. She knew that voice.

"Thaddeus?"

No response.

"Thaddeus!"

This time he heard her. He squatted down and looked in at her. "Letta?" he said.

"Yes, Thaddeus. It's me."

He put his head to one side and frowned. "Why you prison?"

"That doesn't matter now, Thaddeus," she said. "You have to listen to me."

"I listen," he said, brown eyes round and serious.

"Is your dada a gavver?"

The boy nodded. "Yes."

A gavver who sent his son to a hedge school.

"Can you bring him here, Thaddeus, to talk to me?"

The little boy nodded again. "I go," he said and started to stand.

"Wait!" Letta said.

He squatted down again.

"Quietly, Thaddeus," Letta said. "Talk to your dada quietly. It has to be a secret. No one else can hear."

"Like hedge school?" he said.

Letta smiled. "Just like that," she said.

And then he was gone. She could hear his feet running across the tar. She knew she was taking a chance. Maybe the father knew nothing about the hedge school. Maybe the mother had sent Thaddeus secretly. Would he be able to relay the message without someone hearing? She paced the cell, her thoughts in chaos. And all the time there were Finn and Marlo. Had the gavvers killed them? Were they in this building? Questions with no answers.

An hour went by and then another. Letta started to doubt her plan. Had Thaddeus delivered the message? Even if he had, did his father heed him? As a gavver, he knew firsthand the consequences of treason.

She heard his footsteps before she saw him. A small, stocky man with sharp black hair. He looked up and down to make sure he wasn't being observed and opened the cell door.

"My name Turc," he said in a voice barely more than a whisper. "Thaddeus father."

Letta felt relief flow through her. He had gotten the message. He had come.

"I need your help," she said. "Go to the Desecrators' pump house. There's a man there. His name is Rosco. Tell him where we are. Tell him what has happened." Letta could almost smell his fear. She touched his arm. "Please," she said. "I know you are afraid. Do it for Thaddeus. Do it for all the children. We can win this time. Don't you want to be free of them? Didn't you want your son to be free of them?"

"Turc!" A voice from down the corridor made them both jump. "Turc! Where you?"

Turc stared at her, eyes wide like a frightened mouse. "I do my best," he said.

"Turc!" the voice called again.

This time Turc answered. "Here!" he said. "Come now!"

And without a backward glance, he was gone.

Left alone, Letta tried to remain hopeful, willing Turc to act. She stayed at the grating, trying to see out. Very few people passed, and those who did ignored her. She was weak from thirst and hunger, but still her mind fought to find a way out, to find a solution. In the late afternoon they brought her water and a baked potato. She fell on it hungrily.

As she drained the last of the water, they came for her. Two gavvers that she hadn't seen before. The tape was put on her mouth. Her hands were fastened behind her and a hood pulled over her head. They didn't speak, and she didn't struggle. She was determined to show them no fear.

They took her out on to the street and frog-marched her

up the steps to Noa's house. She didn't need her eyes anymore. She knew the route all too well. When they finally stopped, she was in the room where she always met Amelia. They pulled off the hood, took off the tape, and undid her hands.

"Wait here," one of them said, and they both left.

Letta waited a second and checked the door. It was locked. A few minutes later, the secret door in the wood paneling slid back and Werber came through. Letta pulled herself up to her full height. "Where is my aunt?" she said. "I demand to see her."

"Do you?" Werber said, and Letta remembered that eager-to-please tone he had used in all their previous meetings. It was nowhere to be found now. He sat in what Letta still thought of as Noa's chair, his long legs snaked out in front of him, his head thrown back. He didn't even look like Werber. He had a swagger now, something that went beyond confidence. "I don't think you are in a position to demand anything," he said.

"What have you done to her?"

He didn't answer for a second, as though considering her question. "Me?" he said finally, smoothing his hair back from his forehead. "I have done nothing. I wanted some private time with you, Letta. And Amelia has more pressing concerns."

"What do you want?"

"I'm not sure," Werber said, pouring himself a glass of water from a table beside him. "I know what I used to want. I wanted you, Letta. I was so blinded by those feelings that I let you escape. I betrayed John Noa." He hesitated, and Letta could see the pain in his eyes. "It's taken me a long time to come to terms with that. After the Battle of the Water Tower I worked harder. I became a Green Warrior, learned to speak properly, until I became Amelia's right-hand man."

He paused as if considering his next words. Letta waited. He cleared his throat. "I am still prepared to forgive you, Letta. You should know that."

She suppressed a shudder. He stood up and came to stand in front of her. He looked her up and down. "We could be mates, Letta. Together we could live here and rule Ark."

He raised his hand, and she felt him stroke her hair. She cringed, leaning away from him. His hand went to her jaw, holding her firmly. "I know that you still have feelings for me, Letta. As I have for you."

This time she managed to pull away from him. "Are you insane?" She spat the words at him. "You disgust me, Werber."

"I disgust you? How can you say that? Letta!" Werber's eyes were on fire now, and Letta thought she saw a kind of madness there. He pulled her close again. "This is not you, Letta. Not the real you. It's the Desecrators! They've brainwashed you. Let me help…"

With all the strength she could muster, Letta pushed him away from her. He stumbled backward.

"I don't want your help," Letta said. "I despise everything you stand for. I could never be your partner."

His face darkened. She saw his hands clench into fists. "You didn't despise me in the Water Tower," he said. "You didn't despise me then."

His face was transformed. She could see the rage playing out on it. "What do you want, Werber? What?"

He took a step, drawing closer to her. "What do you care what I want? And who are you to question me? You are nothing. Nothing but a filthy Desecrator like your aunt. Like your precious Leyla."

"Leave her out of this," Letta said quietly.

"Do you know that I was there at the end? Do you want to know how she died? I can still hear her squealing."

She had to stop him talking. She couldn't bear to hear this. "Why the peace talks, then?" she said. "What was that all about?"

"That was all about Amelia," he said. "She is such a clever woman. She needed to gain your trust. Convince you she wanted peace. Convince you she would free the babies. And you swallowed it all, Letta. Every word she said."

Letta forced herself not to react.

He kept talking. "You have become something of a symbol for the people, Letta. The young girl who toppled John Noa. The Desecrator who escaped. Amelia decided that you had to be dealt with."

Letta could see the fervor in his eyes. She realized how dangerous he was.

"But enough reminiscing. I'm sure you're curious as to your fate." He looked at her, waiting for a response.

Letta didn't move a muscle.

"A court held this morning heard your case and—"

This time she couldn't subdue the words that burst from her mouth. "What court?" What was he talking about? Ark didn't have courts.

He ignored her question and carried on. "The court heard your case and the case of your friends Marlo and Finn, and you were all found guilty of treason."

They were alive. Finn and Marlo were alive. Letta felt an enormous weight shift inside her. Werber was still talking. She forced herself to listen.

"Now normally we would throw you into the forest, but at the moment, we need to set an example. There is a lot of talk of rebellion in the streets, and it is my duty to extinguish that fire." He got up and walked to the wall of glass on the far side of the room. He stood looking out for a moment, then turned to face her. "All three of you will be publicly executed tomorrow in the square."

Executed. A cold wind seemed to rip through the room. They were going to die. Letta's thoughts flew to Freya. What would she do? What would happen to her?

"I feel a public execution is the only way to restore balance," Werber said. "After that, Ark can get back to business as usual." He touched a bell, and instantly the door opened and the gavvers returned. "Take her," he said.

This time Letta struggled. She kicked out with all her strength and was gratified to hear one of the gavvers cry out in pain. "You won't get away with this," she shouted at Werber. "You can't keep the people down. Eventually they will rise up and rip your heart out. If not now, then later, but your time will come. Your time will come!"

"Take her!" He spoke more firmly this time, and the gavvers slapped on the gag and the hood and secured her hands. The last thing she heard was Werber's footsteps moving away from her.

Werber pushed away his food untouched. He had seen the disgust on her face. He was repulsive to her. He groaned. The pain was almost physical. All his plans were for nothing.

She would not rule Ark with him. They would not live together in this house as he had imagined. Why could he never have someone of his own? Why could she not love him? He couldn't bear to look at her again. She would just remind him that he was not worthy. He would be happy to see her die.

After her execution he would choose a partner, someone who deserved the life he was offering. Any girl in Ark would die to be his partner. And Letta would die because she refused him.

His hands were trembling. The old anxiety gripped him. He wished that he had never mentioned Leyla to her. He had said it to punish her, to hurt her, but he didn't like to think about Leyla. He saw her regularly in his dreams. He could still see her, her hair loose, her head held high, singing. She had looked at him, straight at him, as she fell. He could still feel those eyes burrowing into his very soul.

CHAPTER 31

NON-LIST

IMAGINE

TO FORM A THOUGHT, A PICTURE,
OR AN IMAGE IN THE MIND

She had to think. If Rosco had gotten her message, chances were he would launch a full-scale attack. Letta shuddered to think of Rosco and Amelia pitted against each other. Neither would hold back, and the carnage would be unimaginable. There had to be another way.

Her mind wandered back over all she had heard about Werber. *Know your enemy.* Wasn't that what Rosco had said? All she could remember was Marlo saying that he was a coward. And something else. What was it? Something Turc had told them. He'd said that Werber was afraid of the dead. Afraid they would come looking for revenge. Yes, that was it. How could she use that against him? There had to be a way.

She spent hours pacing, thinking, trying to figure it out. Werber had feelings for her. She could have used *that* against him. Too late now. There had been no compassion for her once she had said her piece. She tried now to dwell on what he'd said about Leyla. He had been there at her execution. Another nugget of information. He had been there. Letta spent the rest of the night pacing her cell, making plans and discarding them until she was exhausted.

As the dawn broke, she called on all the people she had loved. Her parents, Benjamin, Marlo, Finn, Edgeware, Leyla. Even their names gave her comfort. She was afraid to die, but she vowed that she would face whatever came with dignity. And she would have Marlo and Finn beside her. She was the wordsmith, she told herself. She had to show people that freedom was worth dying for.

She was cold and shivering. Her teeth started to chatter, and no matter how she tried, she couldn't stop it. She put her arms around her body and hugged herself. Suddenly, she was filled with thoughts of Leyla. Her singing. Her playing the saxophone. Her gentle voice. It felt almost as though she were right there beside her, and Letta felt stronger.

She was standing when they came to collect her. Standing and singing, just like her aunt had done before her.

CHAPTER 32

#12

DEATH

END OF LIFE

As she walked out of the cell, Letta heard six bells sounding. The gavvers hadn't bothered to cover her face or tie her hands or gag her mouth. It was a dark morning with only a hint of dawn in the sky. A soft mist blew in her face, droplets of moisture spraying her skin and hair. She wanted to open her mouth and drink in the rain as she had done many times as a child. A wave of sadness hit her. She loved her life, even with all its challenges and restrictions. She loved mist and cool winds. And she loved Marlo. She wished she had met him sooner, known him longer.

They walked her down from the Round House to the square, where Werber used to distribute the water allowance. As they turned the corner, Letta could see a wooden platform had been erected in the middle of the space. It was a wide, raised platform with steps leading up to it and three gallows, each with a thick rope attached and each with a noose tied at the end. Every other scrap of ground was taken up with people. People packed so tightly they were touching one another. Men, women, and children.

The horizon was lost in the mist. It felt like this was all there was, this crowd of humanity between buildings and trees. The crowd murmured when they saw Letta, a low hum like the tide coming in on a stony beach. Letta wasn't sure whether it was a supportive sound or not. Up on the platform, a young gavver pulled a lever, and the front section of the boarding under the nooses collapsed with a bang. Then he pushed the lever back and the boarding rose into place again.

Marlo and Finn were taken onto the platform, each one with gavvers on either side. Both men's faces were bruised, their eyes blackened and their lips cut. Letta's heart gave a few juddering beats when she saw Marlo. She wanted to reach out and touch him, take all his pain away. An ache in her throat promised to undo her, but she took a deep breath and walked on. The gavvers thrust her onto the platform, placing her between Marlo and Finn, and stood behind her.

"You all right?" Marlo said with a weak smile.

"Not too bad," Letta said. "I'm happy to see you two are still alive." She tried to return his smile.

Finn took her hand and squeezed it. She took Marlo's hand.

A disturbance behind them made Letta turn her head to see Werber on horseback cutting a path through the crowd. His head was thrown back, and he carried a whip in his left hand. The crowd parted in front of him, and those who didn't move quickly enough felt the sting of the whip as he passed.

Gavvers took the reins from him. He climbed down. He scrambled onto the platform and, ignoring the three captives, turned to the audience. A cheer, led by the gavvers, filled the square.

"Friends!" he said. "Today black day for Ark. Today criminals bring us here. Desecrators!"

There was a muffled cheer from the crowd.

"Ark more important than Desecrators. Desecrators must die!"

Again, the gavvers led a cheer from the crowd, though Letta felt their hearts weren't in it.

"Words not important," Werber went on. "Only word that matters is *obey*! Work hard. Follow orders." He thrust his fist in the air. "Ark!" he shouted, and this time the crowd responded.

"Ark!"

The platform vibrated. Letta could feel the tremor of the crowd through her feet. Marlo squeezed her hand.

Werber strode over to her. Every inch of him was palpitating with self-importance. "Well, wordsmith," he said. "You are not so clever now."

Letta examined the handsome face, the thick lips, the blond hair. She braced herself and leaned in toward him. "I feel sorry for you, Werber," she said gently.

"Sorry for me?" He pulled back as though she had slapped him.

She kept looking at him, trapping him like a moth in a flame. She spoke again, softly so that he had to lean in to hear. "I saw Leyla in my cell last night. She is coming for you."

For a second, Werber's mask slipped and Letta saw nothing but raw fear. "Leyla is dead," he spluttered. "You are lying." No arrogance now. She was close enough to see that his bottom lip was trembling.

"Am I?" Letta said. "Are you sure, Werber?"

Werber glared at her, his eyes burning with conviction. "Kill them!" he shouted at the gavvers.

Letta felt herself being hauled away from Marlo and Finn. "Don't let them do this to you!" Letta roared at the crowd. "Rise up! You don't have to live like this. You are not animals. You are human. You have the right to speak. You have the right to think! You are better than this!"

She felt the noose drop over her head. The rough hemp lay against the tender skin of her neck. But she kept talking. "Is this what you want for your children? Is this to be your future? Life is precious. Don't let them corrupt it. Live as you were meant to live!"

A gavver thrust his hand over her mouth, cutting off the flow of words.

"Kill them!" Werber shouted again.

Letta managed to draw back her foot and kicked the man holding her as hard as she could. Turning, she jabbed two fingers into his eyes and yanked the rope from her neck.

"Letta!"

The voice came from her right.

Letta looked. It was Rosco, wearing a knit hat pulled down low, almost covering his eyes. He held out his hand to her. She hesitated. She couldn't leave Finn and Marlo. Her eyes scanned the crowd, and she began to see more and more of Rosco's people, more and more Creators.

Beside her, she saw Marlo and Finn wrestle with the men holding them, and then all was chaos. Werber jumped from the platform, scrambled onto his horse, and galloped away. All over the square, men and women were fighting hand to hand. The noise was like a wave growing with terrible ferocity. Gavvers were pouring in from all sides, and Rosco was shouting instructions to his people. Someone had given him a horse, and he was lashing out at the gavvers who pursued him.

A gavver grabbed Letta by the throat and lifted her off her feet. The pain was instant and unbearable. She struggled to kick out. Her hands grabbed his hands, but the stranglehold only intensified. Black dots swam before her eyes, and she could feel herself beginning to lose consciousness, and then

Marlo was in front of her, eyes flashing, fist clenched. She fell to the platform, and above her head, Marlo and the gavver were wrestling, and then the gavver was on the platform. Marlo caught her hand and pulled her to her feet. Rosco galloped up, a second horse on a rein beside him. He handed Marlo the reins. Marlo took them and jumped on the horse's back. Letta scrambled on behind him.

"Go!" Rosco shouted, and Letta saw him thrust a gun into Marlo's hands.

Letta hung on as they tore out of the square, trying to avoid knocking people down as they went. Marlo turned the horse and headed up the hill from the square. It had started to rain, fat raindrops that multiplied quickly until the water was lashing down. The horse slowed a little as the rain came on, nervous of the greasy cobbles.

As they came into Moon Street, Letta could see groups of people fighting. Shopkeepers tackling gavvers, children throwing stones, and the occasional bright light as a bullet was fired. As they passed the tanner's shop, Letta saw a hefty-looking man lurch from a doorway. His florid face was glowing in the new light of the morning, and Letta saw the hatred written there. He pointed at her and roared. "Wordsmith! Desecrator!"

Letta turned her face away, but it was too late. She could hear a roar of angry voices spreading. "Wordsmith!"

Marlo cursed under his breath. He drove the horse harder and Letta clung to him, trying not to get thrown off. As they turned the corner into Long Lane, Letta looked over her shoulder to see that the large man had found a gavver on horseback, and that horse was now chasing after them. Marlo's horse raced up through the last of the small streets and out toward the open fields. The horse was fresh and fast. But the other horse was fast too. The rain had grown heavier, but when Letta looked back, she could see that the gavver was gaining on them. As she looked at him, the gavver raised a hand, pointing in Letta's direction. Letta couldn't see what it was until the hand jerked and a bright light erupted.

Marlo leaned around her and extended his own hand. Another loud report, a bright flash, and the gavver was on the ground. Marlo slowed a little, and the gavver's horse shot past them, riderless.

Marlo turned their horse. As they passed the gavver lying on the ground, he slowed further. The gavver groaned, and Letta could see the smoldering hole in the shoulder of his jacket.

They trotted on, past the Goddess statue and down the hill into the town.

Marlo didn't stop the horse until they reached the wordsmith's shop. It was surrounded by Rosco's army, all carrying weapons. Rosco himself was there to meet them. "Get inside," he said, "and stay out of sight."

"I want to help," Letta said. "I can fight."

"You're safer here," Rosco said. "We're going to win this thing, Letta. And we'll need you when it's all over."

He pulled her down off the horse into the arms of a soldier who took her in off the street and through the shop door.

She was surprised to see Mrs. Pepper and Turc there with more people that she didn't know. They were all bustling around, setting up tables, taking guns out of bags, filling bottles with water.

"We're making this our base," Mrs. Pepper said when she saw her.

Letta looked straight at Turc. She caught his arm. "Thank you," she said. "Except for you, we would all be dead."

Mrs. Pepper handed her a bottle of water and a bowl of soup. "Eat," she said. "You will need your strength. We thought you were done for this time."

"Rosco says we're going to win, Mrs. Pepper."

"I think we probably will," the older woman said. "But at what cost? Amelia will never surrender, nor will Rosco. A lot of people will die today." Letta saw the sadness on Mrs. Pepper's face. Sadness and anger too. "We have already lost too many," she said. "People like Rosco don't always count the cost."

Letta said nothing, but Mrs. Pepper was right. They couldn't leave this in Rosco's hands.

"Freya is inside," Mrs. Pepper said. "She got here last night. She'll give you dry clothes."

Letta hurried through the shop and into the back

room. Freya was there, pulling clothes from a large trunk. She dropped everything when she saw her daughter. "Letta!" She pulled her into her arms. "I was so afraid that they had killed you," she said.

"I know," Letta whispered. "But I'm fine. We need to do something, Mama. Something to stop all of this. People are dying."

"But what can we do?" Freya asked.

"I'm not sure yet," Letta said. "We need a plan."

"Am I part of this plan?" Marlo's voice made her jump. She hadn't seen him come in.

"Of course," she said with a smile.

Now that she had their attention, she marshaled her thoughts. She had no great skill at fighting, but maybe she could concoct a way to minimize the bloodshed. All that day and through the night she discussed it with Marlo and Freya.

"Werber is the weak link," she said. "I'm sure of that. People say he is losing his mind. He goes around muttering about the dead. You saw him today, Marlo, when I mentioned Leyla. We can use that—use it against him."

"How?" Marlo said.

Letta looked at Freya, her face lit by the dawn light seeping through the window, and suddenly she knew what to do.

"They don't know anything about Freya," she said.

"Remember how I thought she was Leyla? I thought it, and I knew Leyla. I knew her a lot better than Werber did."

Freya nodded slowly. "And Werber is afraid of the dead."

"Exactly!" Letta said. Quickly, she explained her idea, words tripping out, one over the other, in her excitement.

"It's risky," Marlo said when she finished talking.

"I know," Letta said. "But I really believe it could work. What do you think, Freya? Could you do it? You would be putting your own life on the line."

Freya drew herself up to her full height. "I'd happily lay down my life to stop this carnage," she said.

Letta's heart filled with love for her. After all Freya had been through, she was still prepared to fight.

For the next hour, as the sun came up, they went over the plan, with Letta drawing on all she knew about Werber.

"The first thing is to get a message to Amelia," Letta said.

"Turc," Marlo said. "We can send Turc."

"But what message?" Freya asked. "What message will she heed?"

Letta paced the floor, thinking. "We'll tell her we wish to stop the bloodshed. Say we have a proposal. Tell her we will speak only to Werber. She's not able to leave the house, I imagine. No gavvers. Marlo and I will meet with him, unarmed, without soldiers."

"You think that will work?" Marlo said doubtfully.

"We have to terrify him," Letta said.

"I'll speak to Turc," Marlo said. "Make him see that Amelia has to call off the gavvers." He hurried out.

When he was gone, Freya gripped Letta's arm. "This is it," she said. "This will be a day to remember in Ark no matter what happens."

The next two hours were some of the worst Letta had ever endured. Turc delivered the message. He reported that Werber had looked interested, particularly when he heard Letta would be there. They had asked to meet on the beach at exactly five bells. The light would be dying then, and that could only help them.

They rehearsed the plan again. It all hinged on Letta being able to convince Werber that he was seeing Leyla. The weight of that responsibility was not lost on her.

When the time came, she and Marlo stepped out onto the street. Freya would follow. Their escorts, four of Rosco's men, pressed close to them. All around them were the sound and smell of battle. In the distance they could hear intermittent gunshots. Their bodyguards hustled them through the streets, ducking and dodging bodies, some locked in combat, others just trying to get out of the way. After what seemed like an eternity, they reached the path leading down to the beach. There, the soldiers left Marlo and Letta, who continued on down the path. At the first bend, Letta stopped. She couldn't believe what she was seeing. Amelia was sitting in her wheelchair on the beach below them. Werber stood beside her looking up at them.

"Amelia!" Letta whispered.

"She's not quite finished, then," Marlo said.

Letta's heart skipped in her chest. She hadn't expected Amelia. Her plan was already falling apart. Nonetheless, there was no turning back now.

CHAPTER 33

497

FIRE

(1) HEAT, LIGHT, FLAMES
CAUSED BY BURNING
(2) TO LET GO FROM JOB

Amelia sat hunched, wrapped in blankets. An oxygen tank was strapped to the frame of the chair, and she held the mask in her hands. Beside her, Werber stood, dressed in gray, the somber tone matching the steely waves behind him. Out on the horizon, dark clouds were piled up heavy with malice. Letta could feel Marlo's hand in hers as she walked, and she imagined his pulse beating in time with hers. This could very well be the end for all of them. She had been ready to die when they put the noose around her neck, and she was ready to die now. But she didn't want to leave Marlo. Not yet. She squeezed his hand.

With all her soul, she hoped this was a time for words. Long ago, Noa said that man was the only one who could take an idea from his head and place it in another person's without the use of a knife. That was what she had to do. Place an idea in Werber's head and hope that Amelia wouldn't be able to control him.

"Letta!" Werber said as she approached. "I thought I had seen the last of you."

Letta ignored him and looked into Amelia's sightless eyes. There was no emotion there, nothing but a distant coldness. She turned her attention to Werber. "We've come to discuss terms," she said.

Werber laughed. "Terms? Our men are armed and well trained. They will mow you vermin down. Those are the terms."

"You know that's not true, Werber. The Creators are matching you, blow for blow. We have taken half the town. Half of Ark now fights alongside us. But there has been too much bloodshed. We—"

Werber didn't wait for her to finish. Rage twisted his features. "Blood?" he said. "Any bloodshed is your fault. It didn't have to be like this. I offered you a chance to rule with me. A chance to avoid all of this. But you threw it back in my face. I wasn't good enough for you. Werber the water man. Werber the third child. None of that was good enough for you, a filthy Desecrator. Don't blame me for the bloodshed, Letta. Blame yourself!"

"This is not the time for blame, Werber. You are going to lose. But we can stop this madness before more people die."

"They deserve to die." Amelia said.

Letta jumped. She had almost forgotten her aunt was there. "You don't mean that," she said.

"Of course I mean it," Amelia said, spitting the words at her. "You and that rabble have destroyed everything John and I created. You will drag Ark back into the days of lies and false promises. Even if we lose, we will take you with us."

"No, Amelia! We will give the people freedom and a sense of dignity, which you took from them. They need words. Without words there are no ideas. No creativity. That is what makes us human. You have tried to reduce us—to make us less than we can be."

"Arrogance!" Amelia shot the word at her. "Why do you think that you are more important than the animals?"

"Because I can think," Letta said softly. "I am aware of myself living and dying on this planet. It doesn't make me more important, but it makes me human. You can't take that away from us. What you want for the planet is despicable."

Amelia laughed, triggering a bout of coughing. "Despicable?" she said when she regained control. "You don't know what that word means."

"I know your time is up, Amelia. The people have risen. You can't go back to the way things were. The Creators have won."

Amelia smiled. "But haven't you forgotten something, Letta?"

Letta waited as the cold wind whipped her hair back off her face.

"The babies! The infants you were so worried about."

"The babies?"

"I told you I'd moved them. I have your precious babies under lock and key in the Round House. You remember those cells, Letta? They are inclined to get very damp."

Letta remembered the pools of water on the floor of the cell where they had held her.

Amelia was talking again, ragged air rasping through her words. "A pipe connects the cells to the Water Tower. A set of sluice gates keeps the water out or lets it in, as we desire. Now seems like an ideal time to let the water have its way." Amelia paused, sucking in oxygen.

Letta had heard stories of prisoners being drowned in those cells, but she hadn't realized Amelia had done it on purpose. She heard Marlo gasp. Letta looked at him and saw her own fear mirrored in his eyes.

Amelia continued to suck oxygen through the mask, a hungry sound. "My lungs are flooding, Letta. The Green Warriors have told me that at the end I will drown. Isn't that a very satisfying conclusion? I drown and the babies drown too. Unless, of course, you are prepared to see sense and lay down your arms."

Amelia was capable of anything. Those children meant nothing to her. Nothing.

"You need to decide, Letta," Amelia said. "You can save them or let them die. We don't have much time. In fact, you have no time at all. Werber!" Her voice was like a whip. Werber jumped. "Time to light the flame."

"What are you saying?" Marlo's voice was tight and strained.

"You are not very observant, Letta," Amelia said, ignoring him. "Did you not notice our bonfire?"

Letta looked around. About fifty strides away, a stack of kindling stood waiting. She had walked right past it.

"Werber here is going to light it," Amelia said. "When the gavvers at the top of the cliff see it, they will give the signal, the sluice gates will open, and the entire basement of the Round House will flood. Do you really want that on your conscience?"

Marlo gripped Letta's hand. "He'll have to go through me first," he said, moving toward Werber.

"Get back!" Werber pulled a gun from his belt. "Get back or I'll shoot you."

Letta put up her hand. "Wait, Werber," she said. "There is no need for this. We can start again. A new beginning."

"Do it, Werber. Light the fire," Amelia hissed.

Letta took a step toward Werber. She saw that he could barely wait to carry out Amelia's orders. Words burst from him in a torrent of rage. "There will be no new start for you and the Desecrators, Letta, only..."

The blood drained from his face. He took a step back. The gun dropped from his hand. He took another step, stumbling, his face contorted. He held out a trembling hand, pointing at something behind her. "No!" The word came out as a strangled sob.

Letta turned and followed his gaze. Freya was walking across the sand, barefoot, hair flowing around her shoulders, singing softly. Letta had forgotten about her. Amelia's words had sent everything else out of her mind.

She looked back at Werber.

He wasn't seeing Freya.

He was seeing Leyla, just as Letta had done that day at the baby farm.

"Leyla!"

Letta rounded on him. "I told you the dead would not stay buried, Werber. They are coming for you. You have to save the babies. You will have no peace until you do."

Werber stumbled again and fell to his knees, his eyes wide with shock, his mouth trembling.

"What's happening?" Amelia's voice cut through the silence.

"It's Leyla…Leyla, back from the dead." Werber struggled to get the words out, his eyes never leaving Freya's face.

"Leyla is dead, you fool!" Amelia screamed. "Is that what I gave you words for? So that you can talk nonsense? Light the fire! Light it!"

But Werber didn't move. He was transfixed, his eyes on Freya. Amelia's head turned from side to side, trying to hear something that would explain to her what was happening.

As though on cue, Freya stretched out a long, white arm toward Werber. The light was fading, and the gray mist that clung to everything added to the illusion. Letta thought she had never seen a more terrifying sight.

"Please…" Werber stammered, pure terror written across his features. "Please…"

"Light the fire, Werber! Light it!" Letta could hear the desperation in Amelia's voice. Her words were having no effect.

"I can't," Werber gasped. "I can't."

And then Amelia stood up. She dragged herself out of the chair and started to walk toward Letta, searching for the bonfire. Letta could see the desperation on her face. She took one step, then another, her hands out in front of her, her sightless eyes turned up toward the sky, her breathing loud and ragged. Letta watched as, in slow motion, Amelia swayed, then toppled, falling flat on her face in the sand. Letta rushed to her side. She fell on her knees and rolled Amelia onto her back. She held her hand over the other woman's mouth and nose. Nothing. She grabbed her wrist and felt for a pulse. Nothing. She saw Amelia's face relax, all strain gone from it. Letta looked up at Marlo. He raised an eyebrow. Letta shook her head.

CHAPTER 34

NON-LIST

HUMAN

HAVING TO DO WITH OR
BEING PART OF PEOPLE

Marlo moved to grab Werber and take him away. Letta barely noticed. Her eyes were on the Round House up above her. She started to run. She heard Freya calling after her, but she didn't stop. She raced across the beach and up onto the path that led back to the town. She tore across streets still thronged with people. All she could think about were the babies in that dank hole. Would she be in time? Had the sluice gates already been opened despite what Amelia said? Were the babies there at all?

The questions stampeded around her brain while her lungs were on fire. *Run!* That was all she could do now. *Run!* And finally, she was there. The Round House. The gavvers' base that had just fallen to the rebels. She dashed through the door. Rosco's men recognized her and let her pass. At the last second, she turned and screamed at one of them. "Secure the sluice gates! Go! They're going to flood the place!"

The man took one look at her face and ran.

Letta rushed on. Down the corridor and onto the staircase. Would the stairs be flooded if they had opened the gates? She didn't know. There were puddles of water everywhere. Maybe she was too late. And then she heard it.

A cry. A baby's cry. Tears sprang to her eyes, and she ran down the steps until she came to the first cell door. She opened it. There was a line of cribs and two women, their mouths taped.

Relief flowed through her. Relief and pure joy. They were safe. Behind her, she heard some of the rebel guards come in and go to the carers. She was vaguely aware of the sound of the tape being torn from their mouths. But her attention was on the first crib. She looked in, and a small boy looked back at her. Brown skin and glossy black hair. His eyes were full of curiosity. She leaned in and picked him up. She held him close for a second, trying to imagine all he had gone through. It had been months since he had heard a human voice. She kissed his soft, downy hair. She saw the paper band on his wrist. "Baby Levi Rolling." Then she held him away from her and looked into his eyes. She wanted to shower him with words. To let him know that he wasn't alone.

"Welcome back, Levi," she said softly. "It's all over. You're safe." He looked startled at the sound of her voice, but she pressed on. "Soon we'll have you home with your own mama."

She stroked his cheek and he gurgled. "Who knows what you will do or who you will be? A color catcher? A great musician? You don't even know what music is yet, and it's hard to describe!" She paused to collect her thoughts, and the baby looked up at her quizzically.

"It's like a river," she said finally. "A river that pulls you along and makes you feel things. Love, sorrow, joy. And the force of it! The force is like the strongest kind of magic." Letta laughed. "You'll know when you hear it, Levi. You'll know music and art and all the good things. No one will hold you back. Not if I can help it." She held him close then and kissed the top of his head, the soft hair feathery against her mouth. "No one."

She put her hand into her pocket and felt the little knitted socks she had picked up at the baby farm. Carefully, she put them on his bare feet. He grabbed her finger, holding on to it like he would never let it go, and Letta was overcome with happiness.

She stayed with the babies overnight, confident that Rosco's men were guarding the sluice gates. Shortly after midnight, Marlo came to tell her that the gavvers had surrendered. Even though Rosco's men had been outnumbered and badly armed, more and more people had joined the fight, and the tide had turned in their favor. Letta was glad they had been able to stanch the flow of blood.

By the time morning came, word had spread all over Ark that the babies were safe and well. Many parents had been contacted and were standing outside the Round House, anxiously waiting. A line of soldiers took a baby each and brought them up from the cells. Letta herself carried baby Levi up the dark steps and out into the light. One of Rosco's men examined his name tag and called out his name. "Levi Rolling!"

A young woman, only strides from Letta, jumped as though a bolt of electricity had shot through her. She turned toward Letta, her eyes wide. Her face was a mask of anxiety and of yearning. She looked from Letta to the little boy in her arms. "Levi?"

Letta nodded, suddenly unable to speak. She handed the warm bundle to the woman. Tears were flowing freely down her face as she held him close, the morning sun lighting her hair.

"I didn't think to ever see him again," she managed to say.

Then all about them, babies and their families were being reunited amid tears and laughter. Letta watched the drama unfold and vowed never to forget that scene. And then something else caught her eye. A young couple cradling one of the babies. There was something familiar about the man. At that moment, he turned his head and Letta knew who it was. Carl. He saw her, too, and for a second their eyes locked. He said something to his partner and walked toward Letta. She felt a wave of rage rise to her throat. She could feel her hands shaking. Carl. The spy. How dare he come here? He was right beside her before he spoke.

"They took my niece, my sister's child," he said. "She was

only six weeks old. They promised to kill her if I didn't spy on you. I don't expect you to forgive me, but…"

His voice broke. He looked away. Letta waited. "I don't expect it," he said, looking up at her again. "But I have to ask you. Can you forgive me?"

Letta stared into his eyes and saw nothing but pain. She felt all her anger drain away. She remembered the feel of Levi in her arms. If she had been in Carl's position, would she have done anything differently?

"We all made mistakes, Carl," she said softly. "I forgive you. Go! Go back to your family."

She watched Carl walk away and felt a weight lift from her. The past was behind them. It was time to write new stories.

Letta sat with Freya in Benjamin's old library. The excitement of the previous twenty-four hours had worn them out. All fighting had ceased. Edgeware had set up a field hospital in the shop and was busy tending the wounded.

They had won.

Letta was still trying to take that in. They had won. Ark was no more. Amelia was dead. Werber was locked up. The babies were reunited with their families. Letta had always hoped they would see this day, but somehow never fully believed it.

A voice interrupted her thoughts. "Letta!"

Letta looked up to see Marlo and Finn standing at the door. "What is it?" she asked.

"Someone needs to speak to the people," Marlo said. "They're confused and unsure."

She heard his words, but she didn't fully understand what he meant.

"It should be you," he said softly.

"Me?" Letta said. "Why not you or Finn or Rosco?"

Before Marlo could answer, Freya interjected. "It should be you, my love," she said. "You are the wordsmith."

Freya's words floated across the room to her, and in them she could hear an echo of Benjamin, of Edgeware. She was the wordsmith. If words could bring the people together, she would try to find them.

Twenty minutes later, Letta was back on the wooden platform in the square. Someone had taken the ropes away, and once more the space was full of people, strangely silent. Letta looked around. So many faces she recognized—her friends, her old neighbors, gavvers. And all of them were looking to her.

For a moment she was overcome with panic. What could she say? And then a pair of white butterflies appeared, flying around her head.

At the very front of the crowd she saw Thaddeus. He reached out to her when he saw her, his small face flushed with excitement. "Here, Letta!" he said. Clenched in his fist were three daisies, crushed from his efforts to carry them. "Daisies," he said. "For you."

Daisies. New beginnings.

"Thank you, Thaddeus," she said, trying to keep the tears that filled her eyes from falling. She held the flowers carefully, their white petals spraying out around a golden heart. For a second everything stopped and she was just glad to be alive, to be part of it all. For a while she had thought her life was over, but she had been given another chance.

Could they do better than the people who went before? Could they be true to the planet, their only home? Could they use language to build and not to destroy, as a tool and not a weapon? Only time would tell. Letta looked down at the people and felt the weight of their expectations. Theirs was going to be a hard road. They had to start again. To build a world that would work for all of them. There would be a time for decisions, a time for hard work, a time for sacrifice. But today was a time for words.

She stood up and began to speak. "Friends!" she said. "A short while ago, Werber stood here and told you that there was only one word that mattered. He lied. Today, I give you the gift of another word, a precious word from our mother tongue. This is the word we will build our new lives on." She thrust her fist in the air. "*Freedom!*"

All around her, the people echoed her cry, their voices soaring into the clear air, and Ark shook to its very foundations.

Letta's heart soared as she felt the shackles she had lived with all her life fall away. Words hovered like fireflies about her head. Untethered at last. A whole new adventure lay ahead, and she couldn't wait to begin.

ABOUT THE AUTHOR

Patricia Forde lives in County Galway, in the west of Ireland. She has published five books for children in the Irish language and has written two plays, as well as several television drama series for children and teenagers. She has worked as a writer on both English- and Irish-language soap operas. In another life, she was a primary school teacher and the artistic director of Galway Arts Festival.